IRA TABANKIN

NATO'S ARTICLE 5 GAMBIT

NATO's Article 5 Gambit

Copyright January 2023.
Ira J. Tabankin
Knoxville, TN 39720
Cover by 100 Covers

Dedication:
This book is dedicated to my wife and true love, Patricia.

Thanks:
I want to thank my beta readers, who helped me with their knowledge, comments, and encouragement. I'd like to thank Annis Tilghman (pen name of one of my editors) and Gary Neely who edited and made this edition possible.

Note:
Please note this isn't a politically correct novel. Please recognize that artistic license is used throughout this story. Any tense disparities are the author's view of the story as it's written.

Work of Fiction:
This is a work of fiction. Names, characters, businesses, places, events, and incidents are either the products of the author's imagination or used in a fictitious manner. Any resemblance to actual persons, living or dead, or actual events is purely coincidental.

A Note on Punctuation:
Much of this story is a conversation between people; when we speak, we don't do so in the same manner as the written word. Pauses in the written word aren't usually there when we talk to each other. As such, the punctuation used in conversations is written as people speak, not as it would be in a written paragraph.

Copyright January 2023
All rights reserved. No part of this publication may be reproduced, stored, or transmitted in any form or by any means, electronic, mechanical, photocopying,

recording, scanning, or otherwise, without written permission from the publisher. It is illegal to copy this book, post it to a website, or distribute it by any other means without permission.

Ira Tabankin asserts the moral right to be identified as the author of this work.

Ira Tabankin has no responsibility for the persistence or accuracy of URLs for external or third-party internet websites referred to in this publication and does not guarantee that any content on such websites is, or will remain, accurate or appropriate.

Designations used by companies to distinguish their products are often claimed as trademarks. All brand names and product names used in this book and on its cover are trade names, service marks, trademarks, and registered trademarks of their respective owners. The publishers and the book are not associated with any product or vendor mentioned in this book. None of the companies referenced within the book have endorsed the book.

Note on names.

The names of the leaders of the respective countries in this story are the same, and all of the supporting staff have fictional names.

Chapter 1

I have no idea why I'm writing this history of the war. History, HA! The world as we knew it is buried under radioactive ash and debris. There are pockets here and there of survivors. Let me introduce myself. I'm Major Tom, please no jokes, I've heard every possible joke since I made grade rank. My last name is Morton, like the salt. I'm a member of an exclusive group of survivors of the 1st Armored Division. You may know us by our nickname, "Old Ironsides." We are, no, we were, part of III Armored Corps. We were the first armored division to see action in the Second World War. We fought in Korea, the Persian Gulf Wars, in Iraq, and Afghanistan.

We were dragged into the mess in Ukraine when NATO decided to poke Putin into doing what he'd promised to do. As a boy, I had learned the last battle would be fought in the Middle East, a place called Har Megiddo. The ancient Greeks called it Har Magiddon, it was later translated to a word I'm sure many of you remember, Armageddon. The last battle a battle between good and evil. I think they were off by a little, and I'm not sure which side was the good or bad.

We think of ourselves as the good guys. We fought a war that didn't need to be fought for a country that wasn't a threat to our way of life or to our country. Look, I am, or was, a soldier. I took orders and followed the orders being given to me by those appointed above me, including the Commander in Chief, the President.

I received my orders, and I carried them out to the best of my ability. I helped get my division of M1A2SEP and M1A3 main tanks from Texas to Ukraine. Our mission was to fight and defeat the evil Russians. I was assigned to the headquarters command and reported to Lt. General John Sutton. He was a great leader, having come up the ranks from being a tanker. He knew the M1 inside and outside. He told me he'd spent his entire career waiting for the chance to go toe to toe with the Russians. Well, he got his chance. Not that it matters now, but he would have won had the Russians not played dirty and tossed a few nukes at us.

I remember when I started in armor, I was told inside the tank was the safest place to be on a nuclear battlefield. Now Putin's words rang in my ears. He was reported to have said when he heard NATO was sending tanks into Ukraine, "They melt." Let me tell you, they do melt, and having a few multi-kiloton bombs exploding over us left a torched mess.

Before I go too much further, let me tell you where I have the luxury of writing history. I am a few hundred, yeah, a few hundred feet from thousands that are sitting on the deck of a Navy assault ship that used to carry 1,600 Marines into battle. The Marines are all gone. This 1,000-foot Uber is our ride home. No one knows what awaits us when arriving home or if we have any home left. We have to sail around clouds of radioactive debris. Every time the captain tells us we might be approaching a cloud, we have to go inside, and the ship is washed down with seawater to remove any debris that managed to land on the deck.

I'll try to write what I remember and hope it's inclusive.

@@@@@

The Russian-Ukrainian war began in February 2014 when Russia launched an invasion of Ukraine. Russia quickly annexed Crimea from Ukraine, claiming it was part of Russia.

After the annexation and new elections, the new government of Ukraine began leaning more toward the West to protect them from Russia. They made noises about joining NATO. Putin, the President of Russia, didn't want another member of NATO on his borders. He warned Ukraine not to cozy up to the West and not to join NATO.

Putin spent the fall of 2021 assembling an invasion force of over one hundred thousand troops along the Russia-Ukraine border. When Ukraine failed to issue an assurance that it would not seek membership in NATO, Russian troops crossed the border on February 24, 2022, in what Putin called a "special military operation." Putin boasted that his troops would capture Kyiv in a week, thus ending the "special military operation." Even the American Chief of Staff said Ukraine would be defeated in a week. No one thought the Ukrainian military and people could stop the Russian army. Volodymyr Zelensky said, "I don't need a plane ticket. Send me bullets." He stayed in Ukraine and rallied his people to fight the Russian invaders.

Zelensky led his people to fight the Russians and held the Russians from taking more of his country. By the fall of 2022, he was re-taking territory the Russians had taken at the start of the war. The world was shocked, and NATO said that this was their chance to declaw the Bear that had lived in their nightmares for over seventy-five years.

The world was again shocked when Russia began mass missile and artillery attacks on civilian housing, schools, and even hospitals. Russia also struck Ukraine's infrastructure in an attempt to force Zelensky to surrender.

Zelensky begged the West for weapons to stop the Russians. America responded by sending high-tech weapons. These destroyed over three thousand Russian military vehicles. America supplied surface-to-surface weapons that reached Russia's rear areas. America also sent surface-to-air missiles that were able to shoot down Russian cruise missiles and their warplanes and helicopters. In January 2023, NATO agreed to send modern main battle tanks to support Ukraine's spring offensive. The UK was first with a promise to send 14 of their Chieftain 2 tanks. America got caught in a trap, Germany refused to allow any of their customers who'd purchased Leopard tanks to send any to Ukraine until America pledged to send Abrams tanks. America then agreed to send 31 tanks, and Germany gave its approval to other countries to send Leopard 2A6 tanks.

Zelensky then asked for modern military jets, Poland responded by agreeing to send surplus Mig 29 fighters. Ukraine begged for F-16s, America said no, and was surprised when Poland agreed to send fifteen F-16s. This was the trigger event that launched World War 3. Oh, we'd been warned. Putin said he would strike at those countries that sent advanced weapons to Ukraine, but did NATO listen? No. They thought it was a way to bleed the Russian Bear without having to spill any NATO blood. I wish the leaders of NATO had spent a little time reading history. Had they, they would have understood Putin wasn't joking, and all of our families would be safe and alive.

A couple of fresh butter bars asked me why Russia picked a fight with the world. I told them we should play a game of 'what-ifs.' What would have happened if a country or group of countries had armed the Taliban with missiles, tanks, intelligence, drones, helicopters, and even rifles and ammo? They said, "I'm sure we would have destroyed that country's ability to supply our enemies with those weapons that were killing our people. How do you think Putin looked at NATO? He warned Ukraine not to lean to the West, he warned them not to join NATO, and what did they do? Of course, they got close to NATO. What did NATO do? We shipped high-tech weapons to Ukraine. We showed the world the mighty Russian Bear was nothing more than a paper pussy cat."

Damn, they'd caught me by surprise with their question. I had to pause and think about it. I agreed with their conclusions, we have struck the country arming our enemies."

The only thing Putin knew he had in his arsenal that could scare NATO was his nuclear weapons. He held the largest number of any country. On May 22, our Commander in Chief said he'd changed his mind and wasn't going to send the tanks. He was worried it might lead to World War 3. Germany called our president's bluff and said they were blocking the shipping of the Leopard tanks. Ukraine screamed that NATO was breaking their word and maybe they were a reliable partner. Six months later our tanks and the German tanks were sent.

Putin sent his best tanks and best-trained crews to show the world the Bear still had claws. The Ukraine forces thought the modern tanks would turn the tide of the war. In their initial battle against the Russian T-14 and T-90 tanks, the Ukraine forces got their butts kicked. It wasn't like we hadn't told them the tanks alone weren't to solve any of his issues on the battlefield. Zelensky cried that we'd sent him defective tanks. The General and I had told each other we knew the tanks wouldn't help Ukraine. In fact, they gave the Ukraine's false bravado and led to a lot of dead soldiers and hundreds of millions of dollars of destroyed vehicles.

It wasn't much after that battle that the smart politicians, there's an oxymoron if I ever heard one, believed what we had been telling them. Having the equipment isn't crap without trained crews. Operating a tank isn't like playing a video game. Having a weapon, like having an assault rifle, doesn't make you a soldier. You need training, and I don't mean a few weeks or months. It takes years of training to mold a man into a good, effective tank soldier. The Ukrainians had lots of tanks. Most were T-64s and 72s. They had tanks but lacked combat training. We should have trained them on how to better use what they had. It isn't the size of the stick. It's how well you use the stick. We could have helped update their existing tanks.

NATO had to prove the problem wasn't the weapons but the crews. Talk about a hot Zelensky. He went on air to claim we hadn't provided adequate training or the same tanks our own armies used. Those brilliant politicians took a couple of months to reach a decision on a new policy, so they mobilized us and ordered us to show them how it was done. While the politicians had their heads up their asses, Putin mobilized and called over 300,000 troops into service. I believe it was Stalin that said, "Quantity has a quality of its own." They had warehouses full of tanks. They set up an assembly to update those tanks. The tanks were given layers of reactive armor and improved SABOT shells. A new targeting computer, however, was out of the question because the sanctions blocked computer chips from being sent to

Russia.

Slightly updated tanks with untrained crews against the best NATO had operated by battle-trained crews, and you could have seen this train wreck coming a mile away. My train of thought was broken when the captain sounded the general alarm. We were approaching a radioactive cloud. We had to leave the deck and any other open areas. The ship had to rapidly change course to avoid the cloud. After we left the cloud the captain ordered a deck wash down to wash the radiation dust off the decks. I'll try to write more later.

Chapter 2

A short bit about our ride home. The USS Wasp (LHA 1) was designed to carry 1,600 Marines into battle on landing craft and helicopters. It also carried F-35Bs, the short take-off and landing version. The Wasp landed her Marines in Bodo, that's in Norway. Three assault ships were to land their Marines that would meet up with members of the Norwegian army. The combined force was supposed to cross into Russia and open a second front.

Who thinks these suicide missions up? Close to 5,000 Marines and 10,000 soldiers from Norway opening a second front? Didn't they remember the Marines gave up their tanks in 2022? They planned to drop the Marines off at the arctic front. It's COLD up there, and the cold has a nasty way of dealing with vehicles. The cold also affects the bullets shot from rifles. The air is denser. The bullets don't travel as far or carry the same punch. I hope whoever wrote their orders checked to make sure the Marines had cold-weather clothing.

I befriended a surviving Marine who told me they were outnumbered and outgunned. Marines are the light infantry that takes the beach and holds it until heavier forces arrive to relieve them. They're not the troops you send to pull off a large invasion. Gunny Sergeant Will Stone told me the story.

They did manage to get inside Russia and cause a lot of trouble, something I learned Marines are good at. That was before they got overwhelmed by a large Russian force that outnumbered them six to one. The Russians were so angry that they killed every Marine they could find. The Marines put up a hell of a fight. They killed thousands of Russians, and they destroyed two refineries and six power plants, leaving a large swath of Russia dark and cold. The retreating Marines took a page from Sherman's war book. They burned and destroyed everything Russia could use, that included burning fields and destroying factories. They set explosives to blow up the fuel tank farms at three airports. The resulting burning jet fuel spread like a burning river, it burned everything it touched. Homes, stores, and warehouses were consumed in flames. The retreating Marines left a path of destruction in their wake.

Gunny told me they had a ball tearing up Putin's ass. They laid over a thousand IEDs where they'd do the most damage. They destroyed everything they touched. Small teams spread out into the numerous villages. They roused the residents before they burned their homes. They left tens of thousands homeless, cold, and without food or running water. The following Russian forces were going to have to care for the newly homeless.

I asked Gunny if he was afraid of being called a terrorist, he told me, "After what the Russians did in Ukraine, someone is going to call us terrorists? We woke the residents and made them go out in the streets before we burned their homes, we didn't launch missiles at apartment buildings full of non-combatants. Gunny lit a small cigar, more like the stub of one, he told me, "Have to smoke them to the end, no idea when we'll see any more. Hey, maybe we can make a stop at Cuba, and I can get my hands on a few boxes."

I felt bad breaking the news to my new friend. I didn't know if he knew I was an officer since I was wearing a plain blouse that I took from our inventory since mine had been covered in blood. "Gunny, I'm sorry to have to break the news to you, but there ain't no more Cuba."

"Shit, someone blew up all of those tobacco fields and cigar factories? Did we do it?"

"Yup. I guess the big boys decided they'd had enough of the communist island off of our coast. One B-52 with a belly full of B-83 bombs, each with a yield of 1.2 megatons, destroyed the island. I understand you could see the mushrooms in Miami. One plane ended all of Castro's dreams. The winds blew away from Florida, which is all the puzzle palace cared about. That night real madness ruled."

The gunny looked at the stub, "I guess I better enjoy it since it might be the last one I get." He got up and began to walk away. Then he turned to look at me. "You're an officer, aren't you? No rank tab, no name, that seems to be a spare blouse. I know you're an officer. It's the way you act and speak. You know things a boot wouldn't know. Why are you hiding up with the rest of us? I thought you officers were supposed to hang out in brown shirt country."

"Who said I was an officer?"

"I can smell officers a mile away. You can admit it to me. I won't tell anyone you are up here with us common people who work for a living."

"Okay, you got me. I am an officer. I like it up here. Nice fresh air. I don't like enclosed places."

"What did you do in the Mean Green Machine?"

"I was a tanker."

The gunny laughed so hard he was coughing. "I thought you didn't like tight places. That's the definition of a tank."

"I got out of being inside of a tank many years ago. I was Assistant G2 at headquarters for the First Armored."

"Oh man, I'm sorry. Even up north in the frozen wastelands, we heard about that battle and what Putin did. We heard that you guys really kicked the Russian tanks' asses. Is that why he let the genie out of the bottle? Didn't anyone tell the asshole those genies don't grant wishes, they destroy everything."

He brought memories back I didn't like dwelling on. The cost of that victory was the nuking of our command. I looked at Gunny, "Yeah, we kicked ass. Putin sent his best against us. He sent three battalions of his T-14 and upgraded T-90 tanks. We knew the plan was for them to come to us. HQ placed one battalion of our M1A3 tanks hull down in positions the engineers had made for us. They placed a wall of soil and rocks in front of our tanks, plus they managed to dig up some Jersey Walls they placed inside of the revetments. We sent two battalions to flank the coming Russians.

"When the Russians got in range, our mortars fired hundreds of the new smoke rounds. We didn't think the Russian thermal sights could see through the smoke, but ours could. Our tanks were networked, so we didn't target a Russian tank by more than one of our tanks. The Russians started to hit us with their artillery, and our counter battery radar, the new one, the Q-53, saw its first taste of fire. It was amazing. No sooner had the Russian shells cleared the treetops the Q-53 saw them and calculated where the Russian guns were. Our artillery returned fire before the Russians hit. Our counter battery fire was so accurate that the Russians lost almost all their guns before some even got their first round off. Our shells landed so quickly that their mobile guns didn't have the time to pack up and move to another position.

"Then the real surprise hit the Russians. They'd never seen our newest SABOT rounds. They had just come out of General Dynamic's factories. The M829A4 was a fifth-generation penetrator round. It was designed to penetrate many different types of armor, including the Russian reactive armor blocks. It cut through their armor like a hot knife cutting through a stick of butter.

"It was a true turkey shoot. It was a disaster for the Russians. They lost every tank they sent against us. We didn't lose a single one. That new round cut through their frontal armor, BAM, then their turrets popped off like on a cheap bottle rocket on the 4th of July. Our Trophy defense system knocked down every RPG they fired at us. A big thank you to the Israelis for developing the system, and shame on us for waiting almost twenty years to deploy it on our M1s."

Gunny's eyes were as large as a pizza tray. "What happened next?"

"The Russians made some progress against the NATO armies that had the upper slice of Ukraine. The Low Countries had always assumed we'd come to their aid if the shit ever hit the fan. I don't think they ever thought they'd have to fight on their own. They learned the same lessons the Ukrainians did. Even the best equipment isn't worth its cost without training. Even the Russians had better training. We shared a small supply of M829A4 shells with our friends, the UK tankers who had our left flank, and they destroyed their share of Russian T-90 tanks. NATO high command asked us to share the shells with all of the members of NATO. My general and told the Germans and others to kiss his butt. He wasn't going to share the new shells with anyone except the Brits.

"Together we and the Brits knocked the Russian Bear on its back. They knew they couldn't get around us, so they withdrew to figure out a new plan. Putin lost almost all of his inventory of T-14 tanks, his wonder tank, that could defeat any other tank in the world. He was really pissed."

Gunny asked, "So what did Putin do?"

"Had we been listening to his threats we would have known what his next steps were going to be. He used his trump card and nuked NATO's four field headquarters, assuming that would leave us leaderless. He opened the bottle and let the genie out."

Gunny nodded, "I'm not an officer but even I know after the defeat we gave him he would turn to the only arrow left in his quiver, and he went nuclear. I was amazed he didn't use it when we entered Ukraine."

I nodded, "He thought his forces could defeat us. When we crushed his best, he lost face and turned to the only weapon he had left."

Gunny nodded, He tried to light the stub hanging on his lower lip. "He thought we'd sue for peace right after he used the small tactical weapons on our headquarters. So, what happened?"

"No one counted on the Ukrainians having nukes. They caught the world by surprise."

Gunny shook his head and spit out a stream of spit and dirty tobacco juice, "It's too bad they didn't set them off in front of the Kremlin."

"In the end, it didn't matter. Putin died like hundreds of millions of others when the missiles flew." I looked at the gunny looking at me. "I heard a rumor I tend to believe about you and your people."

"Go ahead, I like rumors."

"I heard you men left your calling card wherever you were."

Gunny grinned. "We did. Our Captain envisioned himself a modern General Sherman. We left a wide path of destruction in our wake. We left nothing for the assholes, and I mean nothing. We did copy a trick from Vietnam, we left playing cards, the ace of spades in our wake. We wanted the Russians to know the god of death had visited them and they were lucky we hadn't come for their souls. We nailed the cards on poles in the center of each village we destroyed."

"I can dig that. I bet it scared a bunch of poor Russians who returned to find they had nothing and they'd been visited by death itself."

"When the word flew, we would kill anyone in our path, thousands of Russians, both military and civilians ran away from us. Our march to the rear, a nice term for retreating, was without incident. We didn't lose a person on our march back to our ships. We thought we were going home, then our new orders arrived. We were to help bail your asses out."

"That's funny because when the birds flew we received orders to get to the ports in France by a date and time or we'd have to swim home."

"Shit. They were really going to leave you there?"

"Not going to, they did. Thousands of us were left without a ride home. I don't know what happened to them. I guess most died from radiation poisoning from the fallout. It kills that motto of no man left behind. I wish I could get my hands on the asshole who issued those orders, but I guess whomever it was shared the same type of death as my people."

Gunny slowly shook his head. "That sucks, really sucks. If you find out who gave the order and they're still alive, find me and I'll help you give them a little bit of their own medicine. I still have a few calling cards left." He showed me his deck of all aces of spades. He changed the subject, "Did Putin escape the mess he created?"

"I'm not sure anyone will know what happened to him. He supposedly had a secret train under the Kremlin that would take him to safety. I know we targeted every one of his shelters we knew about. We even hit the locations we'd heard rumors of."

Gunny smiled. "Why in the world would that crazy bastard think he could get away with it?"

"Once he let a few birds fly, he thought if we responded at all, we'd respond by tossing the same number at a few of his military bases. Remember, he thought we'd match him strike by strike. Tit for Tat. He based his plan on how we were slow to respond to his 'little military operation.' He assumed we would run when he bloodied our nose. He saw how we handled our leaving Afghanistan. Boy, once he hit us, the old man in the White House was pissed. He was always a nasty SOB.

"Putin thought the President wouldn't react, and to ensure that none of his aides could use the launch codes, he attempted to cut off the head of our government, thinking we would be leaderless and couldn't respond. He nuked the White House and Pentagon to ensure he wouldn't get nuked in kind. He bet on heads and tails came up."

I remember the flashes and knew what we'd lost. I was angry, the stupid politicians set up the world to die for their egos. I looked at Gunny, "We would have never been in this situation had Poland not invoked Article 5. We tried to warn them. Then the 'know it alls' decided we could completely destroy the Russian army, air force and navy. All we had to do was send the best to teach Putin a lesson. I wish they'd issued history books to politicians when they won elections. Even our brainless Chairman of the Joint Staffs thought it was a great idea to send the 1AD and NATOs armored divisions to Ukraine to teach Putin a lesson. All because of a few missiles that missed their targets and landed in Poland. The Polish pols got scared and screamed the sky was falling."

Gunny nodded his head. "Up north, we never learned what happened, only the fecal matter had hit the spinning blades, and it landed everywhere."

I smiled, "I was visiting a battalion when I saw the flash and knew from the direction that the mushroom cloud meant HQ was gone, and then nothing but static on my radio. I thought for sure I was dead. That all of us were dead."

Gunny asked, "How did you manage to get your ass on this floating piece of scrap?"

"That's a very long story. One best told over a few beers. I could ask you the same question.

Gunny frowned and looked at the stub that had gone out. "The Russians tried to get us with a couple of tactical nukes, but we tricked them into thinking we were someplace we weren't. Our carrier delivered the mail to the Russians who were chasing us. When we saw the flashes, we high-tailed it out of there. We received orders to go to Germany and then to Ukraine to reinforce you guys. Then the balloon went up, and we were told to return to the port where our ship was waiting to bring us home. We were told that the remains of the Army was joining us and we were to set up and protect a corridor for you people to reach the port.

"Being an officer and all, do you know why our boat is listing?"

"Did you know the Navy uses the same officers as the rest of the services but calls them different names? I was in the officers' mess a couple of days ago. I befriended what they call a lieutenant, someone you and I would call a captain. He told me they'd been hit by two fish. They managed to repair some of the damage, but they couldn't seal the holes, so a number of compartments were full of water. He told me the ship was okay and the rest of the compartments were watertight. The weight of the water on the damaged side of the boat is causing the list. The captain didn't want to counter flood to balance the ship because he'd lose too much speed. The extra weight and the hole in our bottom have slowed our speed to a max of 12 knots, so we're taking the slow boat home."

"Sir..."

"Do you see a rank? Don't call me sir. When you do, every slinging dick with a bone to pick with the officers they blame for getting so many of their friends killed will be after me."

"What should I call you?"

"My name is Tom, that will do."

"Tom, do you have any information about home?"

I lowered my voice so no one could overhear us. "Gunny, all I know is it's bad. They're bringing us back to help the survivors."

"Then some survived?"

"Gunny, some always do. I guess the captain doesn't want to wind us up, and he doesn't want a boat full of suicides. I bet he'll tell what he knows just before we dock, and at this point, I'm not sure he where's going to dock. We both know the Russians surely hit Norfolk and the ports along east and west coasts. I have no idea where we're going. All I know is we're going home. I wouldn't want to be in Europe this coming winter. There's going to be mass starvation. I wouldn't be surprised if they didn't return to cannibalism."

The gunny's face paled, "No shit?"

"No shit. All of their cities were leveled, their farmland contaminated, millions of their people killed or seriously wounded. There's no one left to come to their aid, they're on their own, and I'd bet the bronze age is looking pretty good to them about now. They will have to rebuild from scratch. I'm not sure they'll be able to. I studied enough history to know my money is on small feudal systems replacing the countries we were used to."

Gunny had sat back down next to me, "What does our future hold for us?"

"Gunny, I really don't know. I have zero information on how bad we got hit. If we got hit as bad as Europe, then we'll see small warlords and, like in Europe, feudal systems. They may have recalled us so we can restore order which I'd also consider a bad sign."

"You really paint a black picture."

"I'm only trying to prepare you for the worst case. Shit, we could dock to marching bands." Both of us laughed, knowing I was full of BS.

Gunny asked me, "Do you know how we got hit by a Russian sub? I thought the Navy had that anti-submarine shit down. You know, like in the movies."

I looked at the tired Marine, "Submarines are a bitch to locate and kill. The Russians had a bunch of diesel boats that were almost silent. At least one managed to slip past the destroyer screen and managed to put two torpedoes into this boat, and either it or another one hit a destroyer with three. The poor ship broke in half and went down with most of its crew. A lieutenant told me the helicopters from this boat, and a destroyer managed to locate the Russian boats and sink them. He told me they saw debris and oil floating to the surface."

Gunny laughed, "I bet the European Greens are pissed at the oil spill off their coasts."

I had to enjoy the laugh thinking of the Greens, if any survived, complaining about the oil in the water from the large number of sunk ships and the bodies floating in the Atlantic.

Gunny smiled, "I bet the Green's sharks cleaned up the bodies."

"You got me, I forgot about the sharks the Greens trained to remove bodies from the oceans."

We both looked at each other and laughed till our eyes teared. Then gunny got up to see who might still have smokes and would give him one. I didn't tell him the captain had a map of the country. He'd placed red circles over the cities and other struck areas, I guessed bases, and our ICBM missile fields received the brunt of the Russian strike. I haven't seen the map, but I've heard from a couple of the ship's officers that one exists. I wonder if he also had one of Europe and Russia.

After breakfast, I pulled my notebook from my backpack I always kept with me. I returned to my writing about the reason we found ourselves in this mess. The Ukraine war was one that should never have happened. Our president should never have said it was okay if the Russians took a small incursion into Ukraine. He gave Putin tacit permission to invade, then he condemned what he told Putin he could do.

Putin watched how we screwed the pooch leaving Afghanistan, it all led him to believe he could seize Ukraine and that if he could pull it off in a few weeks, the world, especially NATO, couldn't react quickly enough to do anything to stop him. He had underestimated the will of the Ukraine people and their new president. His information predicting the reaction of NATO and the world was very faulty. NATO watched how the Ukrainians were kicking the Russian's asses, so they agreed to provide military equipment. Most of the burden of that decision fell on us. We were the big dog and protector of NATO, without us having NATO's back the Russians could have walked across Europe to the English Channel. None of the NATO countries without us could have stopped them. The UK commanding general was quoted as saying the military condition of the UK was so bad that they'd need ten years advance notice to repel a Russian sneak attack. What do you think Putin thought of when he heard that. All he had to do was wait us out. He knew the west had no stomach for long bloody wars. We replied on technology and wanted an instant war like in our video games.

Putin had warehouses full of military equipment and the population of young people he could draft. Time was on his side. He knew none of us wanted to get directly involved and as long as NATO sent weapons but not troops, he'd win in the long run.

As of the start of 2023, the "special military operation" had cost Ukraine almost one hundred thousand soldiers, including their citizen soldiers, who were handed a rifle, sometimes a uniform, and sent to the front. They've also lost around forty thousand civilians. With almost eight million fleeing the country, the exact number of killed civilians wasn't known. More and more civilians were killed every day as Russia continued to strike civilian targets. Putin was labeled a war criminal, he laughed it off and continued to target civilian apartments.

As of the start of 2023, the Russians had lost over fifteen hundred officers, including forty-four generals. Many of these generals had been replaced with inexperienced officers who lost lives because they had no combat experience. Our Chief of Staff, General Mark Murphy, said the Russians lost over one hundred thousand soldiers. The president of Ukraine estimated the number at over two hundred thousand. He also said the Russians had been able to regenerate their numbers by calling untrained reserves and drafting over two hundred thousand young into their forces. Many were put in a uniform and sent to the front to be slaughtered by more experienced Ukrainian troops. But time was on Putin's side. He knew the number of experienced Ukrainian troops was decreasing with every one they killed.

In January 2023, Putin announced a call-up of an additional three hundred thousand. This war was becoming very similar to the First World War. The West wondered how the Ukrainians could generate the numbers the Russians were throwing at the conflict. This was the reason Zelensky begged the West for high-tech weapons that could push the Russians out of his county.

Chapter 3

Our State Department and Department of Defense both agreed our best course of action was to supply Zelensky with weapons his military could use to defend themselves against Russian missile attacks and anti-armor weapons to offset the large number of Russian tanks. I had been told our goal was to level the playing field. We didn't want to supply Ukraine with weapons that could reach into Russia. We didn't want to turn Putin's wrath on us. We wanted to bleed the Russian Bear so it would hibernate for ten or more years. We already had our hands full with figuring out how to deal with China. Many thought we were sending too much equipment to Ukraine because China was our largest threat, not Russia. No one thought that if we wounded the Russian Bear, they would turn to China and Iran for weapons and technology.

We initially supplied Ukraine with Stingers, a shoulder-fired surface-to-air missile and the National Advanced Surface-to-Air system, the same system deployed around Washington DC. We also agreed to send Patriot batteries. This is America's most advanced surface-to-air system. We shipped them HMARs missiles, a surface-to-surface system. However, we refused to send the long-range missiles so they couldn't strike inside Russian territory. We were okay declawing the bear, but we didn't want to provoke Putin into striking our homeland. Thus, we continued the war when we could have dealt the Bear a fatal blow. We also should have reached a point when we said, okay, we've wounded the Bear, it's time to sit at the table and reach a peace treaty.

We were surprised when Ukraine showed its own suicide drones that managed to strike a couple of the Russian air bases close to the border. Russia claimed to shoot all of them down. We know from overhead imagery that some managed to strike sitting planes and the runways. The Ukrainians surprised us when they sent drone ships into the Black Sea to attack Russian ships. We scored a few sinkings, enough that the Russian navy left the Black Sea.

We sent them 105 and 155mm artillery. They ran through thousands of rounds a day. They had followed the Russian theory of war that artillery was used to demoralize the enemy troops. Russia used its artillery against the Ukrainian troops, and Ukraine responded. It was a war of artillery. The key to a counter battery operation was knowing where the other side's artillery was located. We gave them our previous generation of counter battery radar. We didn't want our new systems to fall into Russia's hands. We didn't provide them with enough sets to make a difference.

The side with the best intelligence won. Both used drones to locate the other's positions. Each side attempted to shoot down the other's drones. The Ukraine military fired 4 to 6,000 rounds a day while the Russians fired over 10,000. Both sides were wearing out more barrels than either side expected, more than we could supply them with. We shipped so many artillery shells to Ukraine we had to increase production to 90,000 a month. It took us almost two years, but we got there and then passed the 100,000 a month mark. One of the funniest things I'd heard was a Ukrainian 155-gun crew had a problem with their cannon. They used a cell phone and called Fort Hood for advice. The Ukrainian explained the problem to the techs on the base. The techs walked the Ukrainians through the repair over the phone. Talk about real customer service, and they didn't pay for the cannon or shells. Fort Hood could teach any company how to handle customer service.

In the start of 2023, Zelensky finally got someone to agree to send him main battle tanks. The UK agreed to send him some Chieftain 2 tanks. Poland expressed interest in sending him some Leopard 2 tanks, the hitch was Germany had to agree to anyone who'd purchased the tanks from Germany before they could send them to another country, and Berlin said they weren't going to issue the permissions unless the US agreed to send M1 tanks to Ukraine.

In mid-January, President Biden said he would send 31 Abrams to Ukraine. Within hours, Germany and Poland agreed to also send tanks. What the Germans didn't realize was we weren't sending our latest version, the M1A2 SEP, we were sending M1A1s, tanks that hadn't been updated. Those like me knew Zelensky wasn't going to be seeing the M1 tanks any time soon. The armor on our tanks couldn't be exported, not even our closest allies could receive a tank with our armor. There were export versions of the M1. These had to be ordered and were custom built. The versions going to be sent to Ukraine were designed to operate on gasoline versus our versions could run on any fuel. Us saying we were going to send tanks was a game we played to get the Germans to approve Poland sending their tanks. Our President later changed his mind that led the Germans to block their approval, this went round and round until our president finally agreed and the Germans followed suit.

The one thing about tanks and most modern pieces of equipment was they were useless without the right crews. It takes time, months, no, years to train a crew that worked like a finely made watch. This wasn't a video game. This was war where people were hurt, and people died. I and everyone else in the command section of the 1AD knew the Ukrainians thought the tanks were going to give them an advantage. They had lots of tanks. What they lacked, and frankly, the Russians did, too, was training. We train for months against the best. At Fort Irwin in California, we'd assembled the best tankers who could operate Russian tanks. None of us could go to war unless we did good against the opposition forces. I don't know if the Russians had a similar setup. Based on the intelligence reports I was lucky enough to read, and watching them in battle, they didn't.

I'd read everything I could get my fingers on concerning the Russian T-14 tank. I also read that some front-line Russian tank platoons didn't like the new tank because they were prone to break down too often. New military systems take a long time to debug. From the outside looking in, it appeared the T-14 still had some teething problems that were normal with new systems.

Putin showed his complete anger with Ukraine and the west by continuing to send swarms of missiles and thousands of artillery shells targeted at apartment buildings and the Ukrainian energy infrastructure in an attempt to force Zelensky to surrender. Putin was surprised the massive damage done to the housing and infrastructure didn't bring Zelensky to the table. Putin increased the bombardment of Ukraine, yet the war continued. Putin's advisors suggested a massive campaign to freeze the Ukrainians in the winter. They told Putin that surely Zelensky would wave the white flag when his people froze and starved. They told Putin this would bring the war to an end. Putin was very angry when NATO announced they were going to send modern tanks to the Ukrainians.

Putin's response was to mobilize 300,000 and promised a 500,000-man attack in the spring when the snow melted, and the ground solidified enough to support tanks. The Russian Foreign Minister said they would strike any country that supplied arms to the Ukrainians. None of us thought he was serious. Again, did none of the world's leaders other than Putin ever read any history? If they had, I don't think I'd be sitting on this leaking, listing, wanna-be aircraft carrier slowly making our way home. Home? None of us have any idea if our homes are still there, we still have no idea where we're docking. I'm not sure the captain knows where we're going.

Two 'Butter Bars" who had been listening to the Gunny and I approached me when the Gunny to look for smokes. They handed me a gift, a paper cup of hot coffee. That got me the dirty eye from many of the enlisted who shared the deck with me. One of the butter bars, the youngest, I think his name was Harper. He was so young I didn't think he'd started shaving yet asked, "Sir..."

"Don't call me sir on the deck. And remove your rank tabs when you're on the flight deck."

"Si...I'm sorry. Why aren't you with the other officers in the officers' mess?"

"I like the smell of the salt air. I've spent a lot of time inside tanks. I like it up here. No one bothers me up, get the hint?"

Harper asked, "Were you commanding that huge battle between the Russians and us?"

"I was there, was I commanding? Of course not. I'm a major. The battalions were commanded by colonels, they reported to the general who I reported to. I drafted the plans we used to go to war and everything to shit."

"What happened?"

I laughed so hard the now lukewarm coffee ran out of my nose. There goes another clean blouse. The guys down in the laundry are going to be pissed at me again. I patted the deck so the two sat down next to me.

I thought of those initial months when NATO finally found its balls and decided to move in, and finally declaw the Russians. The Polish were the first to send tanks to Ukraine. That initial battle was a blood bath. The Polish tanks manned by inexperienced Ukrainians faced off against experienced Russian tankers who manned T-90s. The German Leopold 2 tanks were the better tank, but the Russians were better experienced and trained. The Russians destroyed over twenty Polish tanks in less than thirty minutes.

The Ukrainian tankers got scared when they saw their fellow tankers getting destroyed. They thought the western tanks were immune to anything the Russians would throw at them. They turned tail and ran. When they ran, they exposed the weakest part of their tanks, their tails. The Russians had a turkey shoot. That was the trigger that led to the madness.

Zelensky said NATO shipped him second-class tanks. He complained to the media that we screwed him with defective tanks and that cost him eighty of his best tankers. The commander of Poland's army was furious. He went on the air to say the Ukrainians didn't learn their lessons and they're not ready to operate modern tanks. He told the world the Russians were in older tanks that weren't the equal to the Polish tanks, but the Russians had better-trained crews which is what turned the battle. He told the Ukrainians to modernize their T-72s and fight in them because they knew those tanks and they didn't know how to fight in west tanks.

While Zelensky complained about how NATO let him down, Putin was sending three hundred thousand fresh troops against the tired Ukrainian troops. Some of the ground the Ukrainians had taken back from the Russians in the winter was re-taken by the Russians in five months. It was a very bloody spring. The farmland was torn apart by tracks, heavy vehicles, and thousands of shells exploding on what used to be land that fed millions. That ruined farmland meant no crops. The lack of those crops led to hunger and massive increases in food prices.

We quickly changed our policies and sent the Ukrainians long-range weapons. One was a brand new one. Some of our front-line troops had recently received a rocket-boosted small bomb. This particular rocket had a range of 95 miles and was very accurate. We thought they'd use them to strike the Russians who'd retaken the land they'd lost. What did they do? They used them for the one purpose we told them they couldn't use them for. They moved the launch trucks close to the Russian border and struck Russian air bases inside of Russia while the planes were being prepared for a bombing mission. Fifty bombs struck the planes and fuel trucks. Half a billion dollars' worth of planes, weapons, and fuel went up in flames.

Before Putin could issue new orders, the small bombs struck a Russian tank staging base. While the small, 250-pound bombs couldn't penetrate the armor on the tanks, they could penetrate the thin armor on top of the turret and the armor over the engines. Over 75 of the small bombs did the most damage possible when they struck trucks loaded with tank shells and the propellant that powered the shells. The explosions damaged another fifteen tanks. The explosions caught over two hundred troops in the open. They were tossed around like rag dolls. Most of those not killed outright lost limbs and were badly burned.

Putin was furious. He ordered a swarm of hundreds of cruise missiles to strike standing apartments and schools. He was running low on land attack missiles so he used S-300 air defense missiles in their land attack mode. He killed hundreds of children and the elderly in a senior center. I looked at the two 'Butter Bars.' "I never understood why the great and mighty UN never declared Putin a war criminal and put motions to remove Russia from the Security Council until Putin surrendered to the World Court. If Putin didn't surrender, the UN would have formed a massive army to defeat Russia."

One of the young Lieutenants asked, "With their pretty blue helmets? We all know their peacekeeping missions have not succeeded at anything."

I nodded, "I agree. Forget the stupid helmets, and they should have formed and passed a motion allowing an international army as they did in the first Gulf War. The UN proved again how useless they are. We should have had the balls to give them an ultimatum to get with the game or get out of NYC and pay all of the fines they owe the city on their way out. Of course, our weak-kneed president didn't do shit."

The other lieutenant asked, "When did you arrive in country?"

I ignored his question. "Do you remember that large missile strike Putin unleashed on Ukraine? Some of those missiles missed their targets."

Harper looked shocked, he nodded his head, "They struck Poland."

"We have a winner. You get to get me a fresh cup of coffee."

I waited until Harper returned with my coffee. The red-haired lieutenant handed me my coffee, "Thank you." I sipped it, knowing it had come from the officers' mess. I like the coffee in the chiefs' mess better, but it was hard to sneak in there and steal their coffee.

"Poland panicked. Russians had struck a highway, they killed twenty-five civilians and four missiles had landed on a Polish Air Force base. They struck four new F-16s that were being readied to take off. The four planes were a write off. Their burning fuel caught a fuel truck that exploded. Over thirty people were killed, and the base was out of action for two weeks. The Polish politicians screamed they'd been invaded, and they officially declared they were invoking Article 5 of the NATO treaties. That was the shot heard around the world. Article 5 would force every member of NATO to come to the aid of Poland.

"The suits who ran NATO tried to talk Poland out of officially invoking Article 5. They offered Poland more aid, more equipment. But the Polish president had told his people the full might of NATO was coming to their aid and would protect them. It was after all why they'd joined NATO.

"NATO was stuck. They had to agree to honor Article 5 or the organization would fall apart. Putin was betting on it falling apart. He issued a statement saying it was a mistake and not an invasion. He offered to compensate the Poles for their loss. That might have worked had the Poles not thought this might be their one chance to completely declaw the Russian Bear and they'd never have to worry about him again. This is where learning history was required reading. The Russians weren't going to surrender. They didn't surrender to the Germans in World War Two and they lost over 20 million in that war. They weren't going to surrender now. They would use every weapon they had to win the war. Of course, our pols didn't study history.

"We got mobilized right after NATO made the stupid mistake of deciding the only way to defeat the Russians was to send NATO troops to man the equipment we gave them, so it was used correctly. Putin warned NATO not to send troops to kill Russians. He would consider it a red line. He warned NATO that if his red line was crossed, he could destroy every NATO soldier in Ukraine. He also promised to use every weapon in his inventory to crush NATO."

Harper asked, "Why didn't NATO believe Putin?"

"That, my young padawans, is the million-dollar question."

Chapter 4

I told the two butter bars "NATO thought that if the Ukrainians could kick the Russian's tails, then surely NATO could destroy the Russian Army. The decision was made to send NATO crews to operate the tanks, and some other of the western-supplied weapons that allies were dumb enough to send them. Then our brass got involved in the planning. They said, screw sending crews to man the M1A1 tanks. Oh no, we'd send our best with our best. So the 1AD was tasked.

"We were alerted, our equipment put on the trains to South Carolina, and then boom, just like that we were on ships bound for the Black Sea."

The red-haired lieutenant asked, "Why would you want to sail into the Black Sea? I thought that was Ivan's private lake."

I laughed, "You know, for a butter bar, you're not half stupid. You were smarter than a certain President I knew. Yup, they sent us into Ivan's private lake."

"I'm sure you had protection."

I smiled, "Sure we did. We had three destroyers and one of those new frigates. The problem with thinking you know everything is that someone is always smarter, and the smarter someone had already thought of it and had prepared a defense.

"No system is perfect, but the AEGIS system is smart as hell, it can knock out almost anything that comes close to the ship it's mounted on. That is until it runs out of missiles, then whoops. The smartest system in the world can't knock anything out of the sky without missiles. The Russians came at us with hundreds of missiles and bombs. The AEGIS caught an amazing 96% of the Russian's first strike. Then they launched a second and third flight at us, but by then we had run out of missiles."

"Then what happened?"

"Oh, we all died."

The two looked confused. Oh, to be so young again. "The destroyers soaked up most of the missiles. Their close-in anti-missile systems managed to knock down more until they ran out of bullets and missiles. We lost all of the destroyers and over five hundred very brave sailors. We were rushed into landing craft and kicked off our ships before they got hit. The Russians pounded our landing sites. The Patriots and the national surface-to-air missiles managed to keep most of us safe. We did lose a battalion of tanks when one of our ships got hit as it was unloading. I'd lost my best friend, Neal Moore, a captain in charge of three tank platoons. He had a total of 50 tanks under him, including his own. We'd entered tank school together. He loved being a tanker. He turned down promotion two times so he could stay in command. I still don't know where he is, but I learned he wasn't on the ship that got hit.

"We landed in country with 338 tanks and 300 Bradleys, and ten thousand infantry. Us tankers don't go anywhere without boots on the ground to make sure no one can pop up and hit us with an RPG. We brought our own air defense division. We weren't going to rely on the Ukrainians to protect us."

"What happened next?"

"The Commander of NATO decided to slice Ukraine up. The northernmost slice was the responsibility of the Low Counties, the small NATO countries. The next slice was the responsibility of the Poles, then the Germans, the Brits, and us. Five slices. The Low Countries, the Poles and the Germans used the same tanks, so logistical support was easy. While the Brits and we didn't use the same tanks, we spoke an almost common language that made it easy for us to share intelligence, and we'd done many exercises together. We knew how each other worked, and we made a good team."

"Wow, that sounds like what the allies did to Germany during the Second World War."

"Yup. It worked then. It should have worked now."

"So, what happened? It feels like we're going home the losers, not the winners."

"Padawan, we're going home as the losers because the entire world is a loser."

"Sir..."

"What did I tell you about calling me sir? Look what you've done. That group is coming over here, and they don't look very happy."

"What are you going to do?"

"One of you go get the officer in charge of the deck. I can take care of myself. Now go before you get hurt."

A monster of a soldier with burn scars on the left side of his face looked down at me. "You an officer? One of them who got most of us killed with your so-called perfect battle plans? Shit for brains officers like you got millions, no, make that billions, killed. You managed in a week to destroy the planet. I'm going to make you proud. I'm going to make you suffer like you made me suffer."

I looked up at his scarred face and saw the hurt in his eyes. "You don't want to hurt anyone."

"I'm going to kill you. I'm going to beat you until you die. I'm going to break your ribs, your legs and arms before I finally snap your neck."

I slowly shook my head. "Are you sure you want to die today?"

"Who's going to kill me? You? You don't look so tough sitting there with your legs crossed like a Buddha or something."

I whispered, "God, please forgive me for what I'm about to do."

"What the F are you whispering?"

"Please take a step back..."

He laughed and reached for me. I shot him with a small 9mm pocket gun I took wherever I went. Both bullets struck him at the cross of his nose and eyes. In the T position. He was dead before his body struck the deck. Two military police officers ran towards us with their side arms raised over their heads. I sat there with my arms up. I held my military ID in my left hand. The closest one yelled, "No one move!"

He grabbed my ID and looked at me. He handed my ID to his partner, who asked me to stand. I noticed both were staff sergeants. The one holding my ID said,

"Sir, what are you doing up here? Didn't you read the captain's orders? All Army and Marine officers are to remain off the deck, and all enlisted people are to remain on the deck? Sir, you're out of uniform."

"Sergeants, this poor soldier suffered serious trauma from his burns and thought it would be a good idea to attack a stranger sitting on the deck."

The officers looked around the deck. They nodded their heads, not wanting to get wrapped up in anything that might land them in the ship's brig. The sergeant leaned over and offered an arm to me. "Sir, if you'll follow us to the officers' area, and sir, we can't allow you to be armed on the ship. We have enough issues with fights breaking out on every deck. Please hand us your gun. We'll give you a receipt, and you can have it back when we dock."

"What's going to happen to the body?"

"He'll be tossed over the side. Sharks have to eat too."

I smiled and nodded. I guess I'm going to have to find a new way to slip on to the deck. One of the sergeants smiled. "I understand you don't want to be cooped up inside, so we've closed off part of the hangar deck and we leave the elevator down so the wind blows in. Even has its own coffee maker. It's got folding chairs and tables. You officers still have your perks even after you lost the big one."

"Sergeant, we didn't lose the big one. The damned fool politicians did."

"Whatever. Please follow us to the hangar deck."

I found my two padawans sitting on chairs, watching the ocean. "Thank you, sergeant. I know those two. I'll be just fine here."

Both of them looked surprised to see me. "We thought you were a dead man. It's very nice to see you alive."

"Same with seeing the two of you. Say, did you know the shit for brains politicians stopped a truce treaty within the first week of the Russian invasion of Ukraine?"

Both and a few others who'd heard me looked at me in surprise. A captain said "You mean we went through hell for nothing?"

The captain's back was facing my back, but I knew that voice, "Neal? Is that really you? Who would have thought we'd both be on this slow cruise ship back home. I was afraid you died when your ship sunk then I heard you made it but information as you know has been very hard to come by."

We hugged; each having thought the other was dead.

Chapter 5

Neal and I found a place to sit in the officers' mess, where we asked each other at the same time while laughing, "What did you do in the war?" I looked at my best friend, one I never believed I'd see again. He'd lost at least 25 pounds, not that he had a lot of pounds to lose. Tankers tended to run lean so they could fit in the main compartment, and drivers usually tended to be short so that they could fit in the very cramped space. The drivers had better be okay with being alone most of the time because they spent most of their time in their own little capsule, separate from the rest of the crew. The only communication they had with the crew was their helmet which contained both headphones and a microphone.

The driver in an M1 Abrams tank used a series of periscopes that ringed his seated position. It was the only way he could see where he was going. Neal's position was not only tank commander but battalion commander. He had to listen to three comms, one between his own tank's crew and the other from the commanders of his three platoons. A typical M1 platoon was 3 tanks, the battalion considered of three platoons plus two tanks comprising his headquarters. In total, he commanded 14 tanks. The third comms line was between him and his commander, who passed orders to Neal and to whom Neal sent SITREPs to keep the Colonel updated on the current situation. It was a crazy job. I know he loved it, but I couldn't figure out how he kept all three comms straight. When his tank entered the battle, he usually delegated his tank's fighting to the sergeant, who was the tank's gunner.

"Neal, the last I heard from you, you were engaging over thirty T-14 tanks. I'd heard you kicked ass, and you showed Putin his new toys were that, only toys."

Neal paused. He held a deep breath, "The good news was, yeah, we kicked their asses. The T-14 is a good tank, but their crews didn't have anywhere the time in them as my crews had in our tanks. We had the new M1A2SEP and M1A3 versions all had been loaded with the new silver bullets, they were a game changer. Every one of my tanks had the TROPHY system. Bless those Jews. I don't understand why Israel installed their tanks with the TROPHY system back in 2011, and we didn't install it until 2020? I think about all the lives we might have saved." Neal looked at his empty coffee cup, he looked into the space above my head, "All of my tanks had the new front armor and the updated fire control systems. The engineers dug us holes so we could hide hull down while we planned an ambush for the Bear."

"Neal, can you answer something for me?"

"What's up?"

"I heard that 40 percent of your drivers were women, was that true?"

"Yup. We were running out of drivers, the average woman is shorter than a man, so after a lot of fighting with DC, they opened the MOS for women. It turns out their reactions were better than most of my men drivers. Also, this is really hard to put in a report. They seemed to sense trouble before we saw it coming. They saved our skins twice by telling us we were about to run into an ambush."

Neal looked at me and smiled, "I ought to congratulate you on your promotion, General."

"Don't you pull that shit on me. You know I was only frocked so they could blame someone."

"Not the way I heard it. I heard you wrote the battle plans that enabled us to kick the Russian's asses. You took over the division after the general and his staff was nuked. You helped save thousands of us."

"I was only doing my job."

"I saw colonels go into shock, and a couple couldn't make a decision to save their lives. I know you countermanded a few of their orders and ordered the mortars to fill the battlefront with the new smoke. I heard your voice telling a couple of colonels to shut up and leave the net. Man that took balls. Large brass ones."

"I knew the new smoke should take the Russians by surprise and give us another advantage. The smoke blinded the Russian's sensors. It gave us an extra dose of insurance."

"Tom, I have to tell you, it was the right time and the right order. That smoke worked like magic. The Russians were blinded but we weren't. Our thermals could see right through the smoke. I watched two T-14s run into each other because they were blind. Then we popped both of their turrets when our rounds burned the seam where their turrets connected to the hulls. Bam, one after another, lost their turrets. When we were done with the T-14s we started destroying the T-90s until they retreated. By the way, tell someone who selected the new 6.8 round. It did as advertised. It cut right through their body armor. You should have seen the shock on the Russian infantry's faces when they realized their body armor was useless.

"I also assume it was you who suggested we share the new silver bullets with the Brits. Between us we destroyed the best Putin had. The Brits didn't have a close-in anti-air system, so we pulled them under our umbrella and decided to merge our units. We could have driven all the way to Moscow had we had the orders, and then the sky fell in. Can you tell me what happened up north? I heard the Poles and Low Counties were losing. How could have that have happened?"

I smiled and nodded, "It was my order to share the silver bullets with the Brits. I couldn't see our relatives hurt because they lacked the best we had. I offered them everything we had and they thought they needed, including M5 rifles and ammo."

"Ah, I knew it was you."

I smiled at Neal, "The poor low countries didn't have our training. Putin pounded on the poor smaller NATO armies in the northern segment. While they had the better tanks, they didn't put in the time training in them. The Russians sent waves of missiles and fighters to pound the tanks and their rear areas. They lacked the air defense systems and the improved counter battery radars we had. The Russians hoped to defeat the Low Countries and then hit our left flank.

"As the number of wounded and dead grew, the Low Countries started to withdraw. The Pole commanding general asked NATO leadership if we had any help we could send them. We sent a squadron of F-35s that tore up the Russian fighters in the north segment. The Russians hadn't previously committed the bulk of their air force to their invasion. We didn't understand why the Russians thought after defeating the Low Countries they could defeat NATO. The Russians unleashed their attack planes to give NATO a bloody nose.

"Our friends in blue used the F-35s and F-22s stealth to jump the Russian fighters, who didn't realize they were the prey and not the hunters until it was too late. Swarms of AIM 120Ds and 9-Xs decimated the best of the Russian Air Force. Over a twelve-hour period, we knocked down sixty-five Su-24 attack planes and twenty Su-25 ground attack planes. Once we controlled the air, we sent in F-16 Wild Weasels to locate and knock out their SAMs. When the threat in the sky was taken care of we sent a squadron of A-10s to kill their armored vehicles and mow down their running troops."

"I bet the next time we tell NATO to pay their share, they'll listen."

I whispered to Neal, "There won't be another time. NATO is finished."

"What do you mean NATO is finished?"

"Neal, old friend, Europe is dead. I haven't been told how bad home is, but my gut tells me we took a real beating. Look at how we're being rushed home. I wish they'd finally fess up and just tell us."

Neal lost his smile, "Do you know why the big genie was let out of his bottle? I can almost see Putin's point when he used the small nukes on our headquarters. We were still winning, but why did the Ukrainians think it was the right time to let their genie out? That was a surprise none of us needed. We could have forced Putin to the table and ended this mess in a way the world could have accepted, and the world would have been saved."

I didn't want anyone to overhear me so I leaned over and whispered, "The world may have accepted a cease-fire and a settlement, but Putin couldn't. He knew if he didn't win, he would have surely been deposed, most likely killed. His dream of rebuilding the Soviet Union would have died with him.

"The world held its breath when the Ukrainians unleashed their little surprise on the world. Fingers pointed back and forth. The president ordered our nuclear forces on alert without ever realizing the Pentagon had beat him to it by weeks. When Poland invoked Article 5 something very unusual happened. Someone in the Puzzle Palace grew a pair and all of a sudden orders were issued. The Air Force had received orders to arm their bombers and to send them to their backup bases. Crews were ordered to complete all of the maintenance to bring as many of our ICBMs online as possible.

"Crews worked around the clock up-arming the Minuteman 3 missiles back to their buss that carried three warheads. They worked around the clock to get as many bombers into the air as possible. B-1s were converted back to carry nukes. Nuclear-capable fighters to our bases in the UK, Japan, and even Australia. I read a report that quoted numbers that surprised me. I never realized we had so many nukes.

"Refurbishment ships loaded with nukes met the carriers and filled their magazines with the nukes they had carried until Bush One ordered the Navy to remove all the nukes from the ships with the exception of the Trident boats. Nukes were everywhere. Before the general was turned into atoms, he asked me how I would deploy nuclear surface-to-surface armed nuke missiles. I told him that I didn't know we still had some in the inventory. He smiled and told me we did and they were in transit."

Neal shook his head. He was disgusted as I guess all of us were. "Tom, think about it, the world is destroyed all because of the NATO agreement that involved all members if one member was attacked."

I nodded, "I do think about it. I only know rumors of what led to the invocation of Article 5. Something about Russian missiles striking a highway and a Polish Air Force base. They the Poles screamed they'd been attacked."

Neal slowly nodded, he looked like he was going to asleep on his feet, "Yeah, I'll tell you the story I heard from a friend in Poland."

"No shit, do tell."

Neal nodded, "I heard we used Polish Air Force bases to stage our fighters and attack planes, so what did Putin do? He hit three of the bases with his hypersonic missiles. He caught us with our pants down. We lost over fifteen planes. One of the missiles missed its target and did strike a highway full of traffic. Putin claimed it was a mistake. He hoped to avoid the Poles invoking Article 5. I think the Polish rightly filed a NATO Article 5, claiming they'd been attacked. They demanded NATO come to their aid. Their president demanded NATO use every weapon, with the exception of weapons of mass destruction.

"No one wanted to see Europe turned into a blackened dead continent which of course is what happened. Damn suits, Putin warned us what he'd do if NATO directly attacked Russia. He showed he was true to his word when he hit our headquarters with tac nukes so why wouldn't we believe him when he said he would destroy the modern world to see the Russian people rise up and rule the world. I'll say something for the asshole, he kept his word. That's more than I say for most of the politicians who ran the world."

I nodded. Neal leaned against the back of the chair to stretch his back and legs. "Sorry, injured my back jumping from my tank. I need some coffee. I'll say this for the Navy. They know how to brew a pot of coffee. Want another?"

I nodded towards Neal, "Don't be sorry about anything. I can't believe you survived."

Neal yawned, "The Abrams is a solid beast."

I nodded, "That he is. I don't understand what happened. Sure, the

Russians hit us. If we were in their shoes, we would have done the same thing. I'd have thought the suits would have turned the request for the Article 5 down. Surely, they knew what accepting the Article 5 would mean. They had to know Putin would see this as NATO ganging up to attack poor old Russia."

I sipped my fresh coffee and had to agree our Navy brothers did make good coffee. I told Neal, "I'd heard it took them three weeks debating and going back and forth, of course, they formed a committee to review the request. Can you imagine if Putin had hit the bases with tac nukes? By the time their committee formed a subcommittee and by the time they would have figured it out, NATO would have been destroyed. Two weeks, no wonder Putin thought we were weak, and he could get away with whatever he wanted to do."

Neal laughed, "NATO would be questioning if they were real nukes and all of Europe would have been turned to ashes before their committees returned with a report a thousand pages long that one would ever read."

I laughed, "Yup, a report no one would ever read, and if they did, they wouldn't have understood a word in it."

I continued, "Putin was very smart. He didn't hit another base while waiting to see our response. He pulled forward another two hundred thousand conscripts from the East and sent them into the meat grinder of Ukraine. He hoped the suits would be afraid of starting World War 3 so NATO would sit on their hands."

Neal shook his head, "The suits never understood Putin's concerns, or they would have pledged to not allow Ukraine to enter NATO. It's what Putin asked for before he launched his war. He wanted NATO's pledge not to expand their borders."

"Want to hear a good one? Back under Reagan, the State Department agreed that if we kept could keep troops in Germany, then NATO had no reason to expand easterly. We broke that agreement very quickly. Putin knew that NATO was a military organization formed as a defense against the Soviet Union. He thought NATO was preparing to attack Russia. How would you feel if the Warsaw Pact had decided to absorb Mexico and Canada and positioned troops along our borders?"

Neal sat back down, "You're telling me that Putin thought we were the aggressive ones?"

"Yup, that's what I'm telling you."

Neal slowly shook his head, "Shit, he should have looked in the mirror. I was trapped in my tank, you had access to the information they didn't want us on the front to know. What the hell happened to cause him to let the big genie out of the bottle?"

"After NATO agreed to Poland's Article 5, we used long-range missiles to bombard the Russian missile and air bases on their side of their border. Putin went on Russian TV claiming his warnings that NATO was an enemy that needed to be destroyed were true. He showed videos of the burning bases and destroyed small towns and villages. He showed videos of miles of refugees that had lost everything they owned because NATO had destroyed their homes. Of course, he never mentioned the damage he'd inflicted on the Ukrainians.

"We should have taken notice that he was making the justification for the use of nukes to his people. The skies were dark with the shadows of the bombers. The old timers said it reminded them of the allies' mass bombings of Germany in the Second World War. We were deaf and blind, and we paid dearly for that. We were so stupid we sent hundreds of planes to bomb the Russian bases and the surrounding towns.

"We played right into his hands, and the next morning at 4 AM he hit us. Small new suns were born over the Germans, the Poles, the Brits, and our headquarters. They were 10 kiloton weapons, close to the size we dropped on Japan. He didn't hit our cities, he hit our troops in country. It was a genius move. He could tell his people and the world that NATO was attacking and killing peaceful Russians, he was targeting only the invading ground troops."

Neal shook from remembering being too close to a blast, "I'm a simple tanker, you're the weapons expert. How bad was it?"

I looked at my best friend, knowing what I was going to tell him would hit him very hard. He wasn't close to the HQ strike, but he was close to the follow-up strikes. "Neal, the lethal radiation radius was just over a half mile. That dose would likely be fatal in a month. Any survivors would most likely die of various types of cancer in a couple of years. The Abrams is a strong SOB but it's not made of lead. All the steel and some depleted uranium shield you from the worst of the radiation, but some still got through.

"One of the mistakes we made in the design of the A2 SEP and A3 was we removed the sealed air fighting designs to save weight. We didn't think we'd have to fight in a CBN war. We didn't think we'd have to fight in those conditions, so the weight saved helped offset the weight of the TROPHY system.

"The weapons were small, producing a moderate blast damage radius of just around a mile. Within that radius, any buildings would collapse. Of course, in the field, we only had tents that were instantly vaporized. Anyone exposed to the blast and flash within a mile would suffer third-degree burns. As a tanker, I know you're familiar with third-degree burns."

"I am. Some of their new SABOT rounds managed to cut through our armor on the tanks without our improved frontal armor. They caused fires in the tanks. Those caught in the fires suffered horrible burns. They went into shock. Many said they didn't feel the burns."

I patted Neal on his shoulder, "Third-degree burns extend through the layers of the skin. They are usually painless because they destroy the nerves. Ukraine didn't have a single surviving burn center. Even our hospitals back home couldn't handle the number of burns from a single nuclear explosion. Many died because we didn't have enough hospital planes to bring them to Germany, and the hospitals in Germany didn't have the burn bed capacity to care for all of the wounded. Those that had a chance to survive were sent home to hospitals that specialized in burn cases.

"Anyone who looked at the flash, and thankfully most were sleeping, would go blind. Windows in a radius of 2.5 miles were shattered. Luckily for us, there weren't many unbroken windows in Ukraine to shatter."

Neal's body shook. I stood to hug him. I knew how close his tanks had been to a few of the Russian retaliation nukes. "How many did you lose?"

"I still have no idea. Thankfully the armor on the Abrams protected us from some of the effects. My infantry who was supposed to protect my tanks from Russians armed with shoulder-fired missiles, all died. Many horribly. My battalion was spread out between 5 and 7 miles from ground zero. I told our drivers to cut all of the governors and break every record to get us to ground zero, so we could provide aid to any of our people who survived. I knew in my gut that none survived, and any who did would be praying for death. I can't tell you the stench. The few who survived looked like the Walking Dead. Their skin was falling off of their faces, arms, and hands. Fingers missing, facial features missing. All were blind, most had no ears, they couldn't speak, they just moaned. I have nightmares of that sound every night.

"The civilians who had been caught in the blasts were as bad as my infantry. I can't describe how bad it was. The children were the worst, my heart broke every time I saw one on the ground or in the arms of their parents. Most were deformed by their massive burns. There was nothing we could do for them. Some laid down in front of our tanks, they wanted us to run them over and put them out of their agony. I told my driver we were performing an act of mercy by running them over and killing them. My driver threw up so many times we had to stop so he could empty his helmet. The entire crew cried with every thump. I have to tell you, it was like looking at Hell. I can't sleep because all I see are the bodies. This wasn't war, this was the intentional murder of tens of thousands of civilians. Don't mention Japan to me, we dropped the bombs to save thousands and then we rushed aid to the destroyed cities. We used the bombs to end the war."

Neal shook while drinking from a bottle of water. "You weren't at HQ when it got hit and started this mess, how bad was it?"

"I managed to take an Abrams to HQ two hours after the strike. The good news, if there is such a thing when nukes are used, was the general and most of his staff were in their beds. Putin struck all four of NATO's command tent cities. He wiped out most of our senior field officers. I bet none felt a thing. They were either vaporized or died in their sleep. How bad was it? I ended up commanding what was left of the division."

"Are you still a major? I heard you were promoted to BG."

"I was frocked, and frankly, I don't know what rank they carry me as. I don't wear any rank because I like to sit in the fresh air, and we officers are supposed to remain below deck."

"That explains why I didn't see you before now."

"Yeah, the ship's police caught me after I had a minor disagreement with an enlisted."

"I think the entire boat heard about that disagreement. If I heard the rumors correctly, the disagreement was ended by a 9mm."

I nodded. "He deserved it. On the other side of the coin, I felt sorry for him."

Neal slowly nodded his head that he understood.

Chapter 6

Both of us were silent, I asked Neal if he wanted to hear story, "All I can tell you is what I read or what others passed on to me. Are you ready for a story you won't believe?"

"Is it a funny story?"

"The UN begged NATO not to respond against the Russian attacks. I was told there was all-out fighting on the floor in the General Assembly. The Russian delegation left the Security Council after their representative stabbed the French Delegate in his neck. He bled out on the floor. The Russian delegates said if anyone else interfered in their special military operation, they would pay a terrible price. The Russian minister said if even a single additional nuke was used in what they claimed was Russian territory, they would respond directly against the country that used the nuke.

"The NATO council ignored the UN and debated among themselves for two weeks while Putin moved over 1,000 tanks, most forty or fifty years old, and another 500,000 troops into Ukraine. He knew we were in a state of shock, and our armies had lost their generals."

Neal looked into his coffee and nodded, "Is then when we struck them?"

I slowly shook my head. "I'd wish it had been us that hit them, had we done so, we might have been able to stop the entire mess before it got out of control."

Neal looked confused, "Well, if we didn't hit them, who the hell did? I ended up way too close to one of those strikes. I can tell you they exploded on the ground. They were very dirty weapons. They made a real mess of the battlefield. Whoever launched them timed them perfectly. They caught the Russians with their pants down. They launched their attack against us with tens of thousands of infantry leading hundreds of tanks. Please don't tell me the Chinese entered the war on NATO's side."

"It wasn't the Chinese. It's a long story."

Neal smiled, "Time is something it seems we have. Neither of us are going anywhere until this tub docks. I'll get us fresh coffee to keep us up, so tell."

"I only learned the truth after we were ordered home. A captain handed me a folder marked Top Secret. I almost threw it away. I, like you had seen enough death to last us a lifetime. The captain told me I should read the report. I nodded and jammed it into my backpack. The captain was shocked at how I handled the TS folder. I told him the war was over and what did any secrets mean now. He saluted and walked away."

Neal smiled, "I can you see jamming in with your dirty socks and then forgetting about it until you reached in your pack looking for something."

I laughed, "Yeah, you know me well. I don't care what anyone says, the note attached to the file said it was to be read only by an 07 or above. No copies were to be made, and no foreigners were to be allowed to see the report. I still have it, it's folded, and coffee stained. Want to read it?"

Neal looked confused, "I'm not an 07."

"The big one is over. It sure feels like we lost it. By now, I'm sure everyone who needs to know knows who set them odd how they managed to do it."

"Can you summarize it? I feel strange reading a TS report sitting here in the open."

I nodded, "Well then, hold on to your ass because you're not going to believe it. It's like a Tom Clancy novel."

"That bad?"

"Worse. The weapons weren't launched or dropped, they were placed along the Luhansk Oblast. They were set along the Russian route of march. The devices were buried like IEDs. And like IEDs, the weapons were remote detonated. The weapons were very dirty. They poured radiation into the winds that carried deadly fallout toward the Russian positions and into the Russian motherland. Putin was furious, but he and we weren't sure whose weapons they were. Both the Russian military and NATO knew they were gun-type by the amount of unexploded uranium sent into the air. Being ground bursts, they were dirty, and gun-types were designed to be dirty. There were going to be thousands of acres in Russia and Ukraine that were going to be unlivable for generations.

"At first, we thought they were old Russian weapons, and even Putin thought they might have been his old weapons, stolen or bought on the black market. It's one reason why he didn't quickly respond until the results of the unexploded uranium were completed. Our energy department offered to test the residue to trace the source and which reactor the enrichment was performed. Putin refused our offer, he said his own people could perform the tests, and if the uranium was enriched in a NATO reactor, he would respond in kind. After a couple of weeks of going back and forth, NATO and Russia reached an agreement that each side would perform the tests, and the collection and test process would be inspected by a member of the other side.

"Here's the hilarious thing..."

"Most of my people and thousands were killed by a series of nukes, and you think there's a funny aspect to it?"

"Neal, please. I feel your pain. I feel for your loss. Please let me continue."

"Go on, tell me the funny part of the start of the third world war."

"When the Russians and we openly compared notes, we got the same results, the uranium was enriched in a Russian reactor. This threw the Russians for a loop. They asked for a cease-fire so they could do an inventory of their old weapons. The Russians never threw any old military equipment away. While we dismantled our old nukes, they didn't. They kept theirs in bunkers that supposedly hadn't been touched since the breakup of the Soviet Union.

"We and the other NATO militaries used the cease-fire to move additional people and equipment to the front. We separated most of our units in case Putin responded with his own nukes. We made a large show of moving some of our own special weapons into the field. We wanted Putin to know we were ready to respond to his use of nukes. I was told to remain a BG to run the Division until the Pentagon could decide whom they were going to send. I think they considered me, some low major, to be a throw-away versus a flag officer. I think the generals got together and decided this was going to turn into a real mess, one none of those ass-kissing assholes wanted to be in the middle of, so they decided to send me into the lion's den. They'd call every hour for a sitrep and issue orders, some decent and some impossible to carry out. Most of their orders, I simply responded with a 'yes, sir' and did what I thought was the right thing to do. I thought I had the situation in hand, and then the shit hit the fan."

Neal looked very tired. "I don't understand, if the Russians knew the enriched uranium was theirs, why the second strike?"

"Here's the real funny part of the story. The weapons were made by the Ukrainians."

Neal sat up and looked at me, "Who gave them nukes? Tanks and missiles I understand but nukes? That would be like handing a baby a firestick. Who the F was that crazy? Please don't tell me it was us."

"Google gave it to them."

"Google? I don't understand. Why did the Russians think the uranium came from their reactors if it didn't?"

"In a manner of speaking, the enriched uranium was from a Russian reactor. Old ones, ones they used to operate, where? In Ukraine, so in a manner of speaking, the reactor that enriched the uranium came from a Russian reactor."

Neal looked very confused, "How did a reactor end up in Ukraine?"

"You have to remember Ukraine used to be part of the Soviet Union. They once even had a number of Soviet nuclear bombers and missiles. We promised we'd protect them if they'd return the nukes to Moscow. See how well that promised turned out?"

"I'm still confused."

"The Ukrainians operated the largest reactors in Europe. All they had to do was perform some research on Google on how a gun-type atomic weapon was constructed. It's the simplest type of nuke to build. It was the design of our first atomic device and the design of the one the Enola Gay dropped on Hiroshima. Of course, Google didn't tell them the formulas for how much explosives were needed to slam one piece of uranium into the other, but there was enough information on Google for their scientists to figure it out."

"Wait a minute. Many countries have attempted to construct a nuclear weapon, all of them failed, how could Ukraine succeed?"

"We believe they managed to get some outside help. No one is really sure who supplied the help. The money was on Israel. I heard some G2 say that Israel supplied them with detailed schematics in exchange for Russian tech and weapons so they could figure out countermeasures. Of course, they've denied any part of assisting the Ukrainians in the assembly of the weapons."

Neal looked confused, "I didn't think they knew how to manufacture nukes."

I smiled, "Old buddy, they have over 200 nukes. Their white coats helped develop a lot of our nuke technology. For example, they developed the neutron weapon."

"You're telling me the Israelis helped the Ukrainians develop a bomb..."

"Not a bomb, a device, a crude atomic device that they buried and exploded as the Russian advance started their spring offensive. Their timing was perfect. They had drones watching the Russian tanks, and when the bulk of the tanks entered the kill zone, they set off the devices. Not even a modern tank can survive a nuclear explosion going off under or next to them."

"When did Putin decide the bombs came from Ukraine?"

"It took them three months to finally accept what we already knew. We saw Putin pull his tanks and troops across the border. It was at that moment that we knew he planned to strike Ukraine with nuclear weapons as payback."

"Did Putin know about Israel's involvement? Did he strike at them?"

"We didn't know if he knew, and to the best of my knowledge, the Russians didn't strike Israel. I know that at the time of the start of WW 3, Israel was still holding her own against Iran, who thought it was the right time to strike their number one enemy, Israel. I learned that Israel managed to intercept most of Iran's missiles and planes. They were the only country with a multi-layered defense against planes and missiles. They were also the first country to deploy a network of lasers for missile defense. No system is ever perfect, and a few of Iran's missiles managed to get through Israel's defenses. Israel suffered tremendous damage from Iran's nuclear weapons that they weren't supposed to have. Jerusalem was destroyed by three of Iran's nukes.

"Israel struck back with over one hundred nuclear weapons. They dug out Iran's shelters with ground-penetrating nukes. That was the end of the mullahs. There is no Iran left."

Neal asked. "What do you mean there's no Iran left? How could a country disappear? Even one hundred nukes wouldn't erase a country the size of Iran."

"There are some things worse than just nuclear weapons. Israel covered most of their warheads and bombs with a highly radioactive element. Whatever they used had a half-life measured in generations. Most of Iran is now a smoking radiation death zone. I heard from the Pentagon before it was destroyed that Iran would remain radioactive for over two hundred years. Israel was ensuring Iran could never again rise up and threaten them again. We didn't know what they salted their weapons with. They refused to answer all of our requests. There were a few theories, and then the Pentagon was vaporized when a nuke exploded over it."

Neal asked, "What about the shelter under the Pentagon, it was supposed to be designed to survive a direct hit."

"No idea. All comms from the D.C. area ended in the attack."

Neal started to smile, "No more D.C.? No more BS mandates from them, no more woke BS?"

"No more woke. Woke died in the nuclear mushroom clouds of death."

Neal laughed, "At least some good came from the attack."

"You know, that's a horrible thing to say."

Neil's smile faded, "Those assholes cost us most of our division, I mean, your division. Sir."

I smiled when he called me sir with a laugh in his voice. Neal continued, "They lost our country, and I bet they also destroyed most of the northern hemisphere. They played poker and tried to bluff without even a pair. They played poker with a world-class poker player who told them he was holding a full house, and what did they do? They tried to bluff their way out. They forgot Putin didn't bluff. They played with our lives."

"I know, but what can we do about it now?" I asked while looking at the grinds in my cup.

Neal stood up and went for our fifth or sixth cup of coffee. He'd gotten my hint. He's also left my question hanging in the air. He knew there wasn't a damn thing we could do about it. He returned with our coffee. "What do you think we're going to find when we finally get home?"

"I have no idea. I've asked the navy pukes what they knew, and they said the captain was keeping mum and not even giving a hint of what's left."

I was about to say something when the alarm screamed, "GENERAL QUARTERS, GENERAL QUARTERS. THIS IS NOT A DRILL."

Neal and I looked at each other. He asked, "What the hell does he expect us to fight with? This ship is listing from the last time the captain tangled with a Russian sub."

The alarm screamed, "General quarters, prepare to defend against enemy aircraft."

I looked at Neal, "At least we have some SAMs to defend us against aircraft." A moment later, we heard the alarm scream, "Clear the deck, missiles launching."

We heard the swoosh of the Evolved Sea Sparrows launch. I counted, one, there goes two, and three..."

Neal added, "Four, five, and six."

We next heard the ripping sound of the ship's CIWS guns firing, which was followed by three explosions. I smiled, "I guess we got three of them."

A moment we felt the ship shake, and we heard the explosion followed by the fire alarms. Navy pukes ran to fight the fire. I yelled at one, "What got hit?"

"We got two of their planes and four of their missiles. One of theirs got through the CIWS when we ran out of ammo. It struck the end of the flight deck up near the bow. It didn't damage anything we can't do without. The fires will be out very soon. Just stay here and don't worry."

"Any idea where the planes came from? We're in the damn ocean."

"The Russians had one carrier."

"Had?"

"One of our destroyers got her with a nuke anti-ship missile. We're still going home, they're on their way to Davy Jones' Locker, or as they say, they're sleeping with the fish tonight."

We thanked the sailor. The wind blew the smoke inside the ship. On the battlefield, I knew I could fight, here, I felt helpless. I didn't like having my hands tied behind my back. At least we may still make it home. Neal read my mind, "Home to what? We know both sides shot their wad at each other. What do you think we're going to find when we reach home?"

"I really don't know, and frankly, it scares me.

"I faced the best the Russians could throw at me. I faced their nukes, I faced certain death. I wasn't scared when I faced the best they threw at me, but I admit, like you, I'm scared of what we're going to find when we get home."

Chapter 7

Neal went off to try to get some sleep. I understood his nightmares; everyone who's been in this war shares the same nightmares. I didn't tell him I had noticed some bleeding from his gums. I knew it was the start of the radiation working its devilish ways through his body. I wonder how many rads he'd received in the nuclear explosions that took place in Ukraine. I hope his body is strong enough to fight off the radiation I knew he absorbed. Rest is the best thing for him. I'll drop by the medical office and have a chat with the doctor. I know his hands are full with lots of people in much worse shape than Neal, but he's my best and most likely my only friend left.

I wanted to go up on the deck, but I was warned to stay off of it. I, like the other officers, was given a rack, and that's what they looked like. They were stacked three or four high. Our only privacy was provided by thin curtains that helped block the light from the common square that our racks surrounded. They did nothing for the noise. I'm glad I and most of us had foam earplugs we were supposed to use when we had to fire our rifles. The administration didn't want us to go deaf and take up space in the VA hospitals they had been trying to close. They worked miracles to block the sound of the ship and the constant announcements that most of us learned to ignore.

Most of us couldn't sleep, no matter how well the curtains blocked the light, and the earplugs blocked the noise. We've been fighting our own devils. Every night many cried in pain. Some woke covered in sweat and with the shakes. The doc had long ago run out of sleeping meds. Someone on the ship was growing marijuana. None of us had any idea who it was. Every evening between 20 and 23 hundred hours, a masked face poked their face in our bunking room, asking if we wanted any. For a little more, they sold laced cookies. They told us the safest place on the ship to smoke the grass was on the stern side hangar deck, where the winds blew the smoke off the ship.

We assumed the ship's officers knew about the grass but kept a blind eye because the ship was loaded with combat vets who were angry at the world. The rumor said the crew of the ship were prohibited from using any drugs. I'll admit I use it every night to help me sleep and not be consumed with my own devils. I don't worry about getting tested when we return. I'm not sure what we're going to find, but my gut tells me it's going be worse than anything we can imagine. From the damage I witnessed in Ukraine from the small explosions, I knew home was going to be a wasteland. Most of Ukraine was desolate before the nukes from the Russian near-constant bombardment. I wasn't sure where the pre-nuke damage and the nuke damage started. Most of Ukraine's cities resembled Berlin at the end of the Second World War.

The difference between Berlin in 1945 and Ukraine of 2024 was that there was no one to rebuild Ukraine or, for that matter, rebuild any of the world's once-great cities. No one wanted to risk their life by entering the burnt and possibly still radioactive debris to rebuild, and more importantly, there was no money. The cities that remain may be no-go and dead zones for generations.

The captain has refused to share any of the overhead images I know he must have. Many of the satellites remain overhead. Though they survived, most of the receiving stations were destroyed. The Navy's ships had the computers, radios, and antennas to communicate with the birds, so I knew the ship's captain had the images. He's afraid of the hit to our morale that seeing our homes in ruins would do to us.

The captain has made daily ship-wide communications telling us we're the future and we're necessary to the rebuilding of America. He was afraid many of us would jump off the boat. He had orders to bring as many of us home as possible. He never said where the orders originated from or where we were going to dock.

I was finally falling asleep from total exhaustion when the captain used the 1MC to announce, "Attention, attention, this is the captain, all officers, regardless of service, O4 or above, meet in the Chiefs' mess in ten minutes, I repeat, all officers, o4 or above report to the Chiefs' mess in ten minutes."

Of course, he'd have to have his officer meeting when I had finally gotten to sleep. I wonder why he limited it to O4. I knew Neal would be all over me as soon I returned. I bet I'd find him waiting by my bunk. I wish I knew where we were, but the ocean doesn't have exit signs or mile markers. The crew have all been ordered not to tell any of us grunts where we were or where we were going.

I was early so that I could grab a seat. The captain must owe the chiefs a huge favor to use their mess for the meeting. He couldn't use the officers' mess because that was one of the few places we were allowed to go to 24 hours a day. Even arriving ten minutes early, I managed to grab one of the last chairs. There must be a lot of Marines on board. They're always early. They believed five minutes early was being late. As the captain entered, one of the do-gooder Marines yelled, "Attention, captain on deck." We jumped to our feet. The captain said, "As you were." We sat and waited for word from the high and mighty.

"Ladies and gentlemen, thank you for joining me tonight. I know I woke some of you from sleep that is hard to come by on this ship. I called you to announce where we're going and why. Most of you were on the front line when the shit hit the fan. Before I tell you where we're going, I believe it's a good idea to explain what happened."

A young man, to my eyes, too young to be a major, yet wearing the rank, must have been a Marine who got field promoted when everyone above him was killed. He stood and asked, "Sir, why aren't you sharing this information with everyone?"

"Son, because those are my orders, and according to the information I was sent, all of you hold at least a secret clearance. Am I correct? Do all of you have at least a secret clearance?"

The captain looked around the room, we all nodded our heads. "Good. My orders are to give you a summary of what happened and what's expected of you and the people on this and other ships."

Someone yelled, "I served my term, I lost most of my people because some suit bluffed without holding a face card. I'm done being a soldier, I just want to go home. I want to resign my commission."

The captain slowly nodded his head, knowing this was going to be what many thought. "Son, I'm sorry to have to be the bearer of bad news, but the terms of service of every member of every branch of the military and the Coast Guard have been indefinitely extended for the good of the country. The president isn't accepted any one resigning their commissions."

A Lt. Colonel stood, a third of his face was scarred with burns, "Sir, who's giving orders? Is there a federal government? Where is it located? Why don't you start with what's the condition of the country? All of us fought with distinction, and we're being treated like children. I for one, don't appreciate it. Most of us paid a price that can't be repaid. Treat us as the warriors we are, or I am leaving this tea party of yours. When I leave, I'll order everyone I outrank to leave with me."

"Colonel, please don't do that. I'd have to order you to be placed in the brig."

"Captain, you are a naval officer, let's be very frank. You command a bus. You pick up and deliver Marines to where they're needed. On the other hand, most of us are warriors. We've faced the devil and stared him down. Your BS isn't playing with us. If you attempt to place me in the brig, my friends will take this ship from you. Don't think for a minute we can't or won't do it. Many of us were trained to take ships like this one. You rely on Marines for security. What are you going to do when those Marines turn on you? We're not fools, we know we have little or nothing to go home to. You need to level with us and everyone on this crate.

"By the way, you'll never get away with putting me in the brig."

The captain looked very angry. His face had turned bright red, he didn't like being talked to like that on his own ship.

The colonel stared the captain in his eyes, "Why don't you tell us what you came to tell us so that we can decide what we're going to do. I don't think any of us can be held against our wills. As far as the government, I happen to know the Pentagon, all of D.C., Mount Weather, Raven Rock, and the Cheyenne Mountain Complex were all destroyed. I was on my sat phone with the Pentagon when they screamed they were under attack, then my call was cut, and all I heard on my end was static. That static was caused by a nuke exploding, and all of the electronics were destroyed. All of the people I was just talking to were vaporized. I lost many friends in less than a second. Where were you when the nukes were tossed around? If this ship had been close to one, you wouldn't have a ship to command.

"You haven't told us shit about what happened back home. We assume our families and friends are dead, but you've withheld any information about our homes. You've got a boat full of angry, worried people who are filled with grief. Most are suffering from PTSD, and you want to play games with us? Most of the people you've crammed into this ship are ticking bombs, just waiting for something to set them off.

"How many fights a day are your people stopping? How many jumped into the ocean or slit their wrists? Captain, I don't think you have any idea of the cargo, we all know that's what you call us, are capable of. These are the survivors of nukes exploding close to their positions, ones they were ordered to hold even though the Pentagon knew they were going to get hit by WMD. We carried out our orders because it's what we do. Treat us as adults who have earned the right to know what's going on."

I looked on with surprise and shock. I figured Mount Weather and Raven Rock would be destroyed, but Cheyenne Mountain was designed to take a direct hit.

The captain slowly shook his head, "If you'll let me tell you why I called this meeting, we might be able to see eye to eye. You are correct, those shelters were all destroyed, including Cheyenne that received four hits with 25-megaton warheads. It was designed to survive one, not four. The Russians hit each shelter with three sub-launched warheads, each at least 100 kilotons. One was set for ground penetrator, the next a ground burst, and the follow up an air burst. The two ground bursts destroyed the shelters, the air bursts pushed the fallout back down, making recovery impossible. The Russians hit Cheyenne with their new Satan 2 ICBMs, each carried one 25 megaton warhead. They were timed a few minutes after another. They were aimed at the same place. The first dug a hole, the second deepened the hole, the third cracked the mountain, and the fourth exploded inside the mountain, killing everyone inside."

The colonel nodded his head. "How did they manage to launch missiles and not get the President out of the White House? I thought the Secret Service practiced getting the president to safety in a nuke attack."

The captain slowly nodded his head, "You're right, but they didn't practice for sappers to smuggle in a couple of nuclear weapons. One exploded in the parking lot of the Pentagon, and one exploded in a U-Haul truck in front of the White House. The Secret Service was alerted to the sub-launch by NORAD. They grabbed the president and carried him to the presidential shelter. A second team saw the truck idling and went to tell it to move on when the device exploded. The Russians weren't sure the sappers would work, so they launched from a sub as their insurance policy.

The sub-launched missiles finished the job the truck bombs didn't complete. The missiles destroyed the Pentagon and White House shelters with the president and his staff. The Sec DOD, all of the chiefs and senior officers were destroyed in the war shelter under the Pentagon."

Everyone was silent.

The colonel nodded, "We'd known the Russians had deep cover agents in America. The FBI was more interested in playing political games and arresting soccer moms than Russian agents. When did they explode the weapons?"

"Midnight. The president and his wife were asleep in bed."

I whispered, but the colonel heard me, "At least they didn't know anything. Not that he knew any shit anyway."

"Can it! We're talking about a dead president."

"Yes, sir."

The captain looked at me, "Don't think I don't know who you are. I know you hide behind a blouse without a rank, and I know you were frocked to BG when your headquarters got hit. You're the highest officer on this rust bucket, so why don't you act like it?"

"Colonel, I have no desire to be in command. You have the experience. I was frocked to be a scapegoat."

"A smart major, I didn't know I'd meet one. Most are happy either playing political games or they're ass-kissers. A few want to get back in combat which is the category you fall into."

"Thank you. I hated being a staff officer. I offered to take over a battalion until a more experienced officer arrived to run the remains of the division. No one came. I received orders to command the remains of the division which is what I did."

"There, ladies and gentlemen is a smart man. Major, I mean General Morton, I respect you." He saluted me, and I returned his.

The captain continued, "Mount Weather and Raven Rock were hit by submarine-launched missiles. They had less than 10 minutes notice. Most of the Representatives and Senators were caught by the bursts before they even left DC. Arlington died with the dual nukes that destroyed the Pentagon. Central Virginia got creamed when Mount Weather was struck. Norfolk went when three sub-launched missiles struck the world's largest naval base. I-95 and 64 were covered in fallout. Based on the overheads, it looks like I-95 received of strikes. The Russians must have been trying to nail members of Congress and the cabinets on their way to Weather. If any managed to make it to Weather they'd have found a smoking hole in the ground. I know the shelters were destroyed, I can't be sure if a ground penetrator was used or not. There's just a large hole where Mount Weather used to be. For now, let's call it a ground strike followed by an air burst."

We sat in shock, we knew things were bad, but nuke-armed sappers was something we hadn't counted on. The captain unrolled a map of the country. It was the map I'd heard about. It was covered in the nuclear strikes, and the long black tails that we knew were wind-driven fallout.

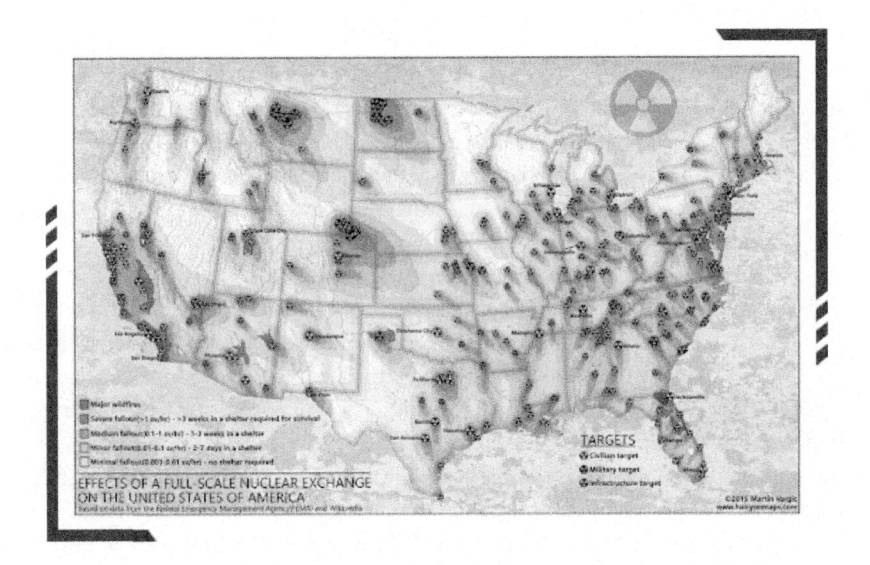

We stared at the map. I asked, "Captain, do you have a similar map of Russia and Europe?"

Someone yelled back, "Who cares about Europe, they started this mess, and as far as Russia, as long as they got creamed, I don't care what happened to them."

The captain replied. "I have maps of Europe and Russia. There is no more Europe, and Russia got creamed about the same as us. Every one of the Russian cities and military bases were hit. We hit Russia, and then France and the UK hit them. There's a rumor that at the end, even China lobbed a few at Russia. We believed that they wanted to stop Russia from being able to stop them from moving into Siberia and helping themselves to the oil and minerals there. These maps are based on our satellites and may not be accurate because of the smoke that covers entire countries. There's nothing left of Europe. Everyone of their cities were hit. There bases vaporized. Farmland was hit by air and ground bursts to destroy the rich soil that fed the continent. The fallout covered so much of Europe the black was all black. I can't leave these maps up. I don't want to further agitate the crew or as you say, the cargo."

The colonel smiled and nodded.

"I told you because together we have a job to do. We have to spend the next few days preparing for the reality of what they're going to find when we dock, which is going to be Mayport, next to Jacksonville. It's the only base large enough to dock this ship. It also has a working dry dock that may enable us to repair this barge."

I asked the question most of us wanted to ask, "What are we supposed to do there?"

"I think it best if you rest after what I told you today, and we'll discuss our future tomorrow."

The captain took his maps and left us sitting in silence.

Chapter 8

A Lt. Commander who had been the XO on the USS Barry, DDG 53, stopped to chat with me. I asked why he wasn't on his ship, he told me a sub-launched cruise missile had sunk it.

"I thought you had anti-missile defenses."

"We did, until we ran out of missiles and bullets for our close-in weapons. That damn missile flew at Mach 3 and right above the wave tops. By the time we saw it, we were hit. The sub launched six missiles, we managed to knock four of them down. The two that hit couldn't have picked a worse place to hit. One struck the forward missile cells, still loaded with land attack Tomahawks. The Russian missile had pierced the hull and exploded in the missile cells. The explosion tore the front of the ship off. The second missile struck the helicopter hangar when the crew was fueling and arming the two helicopters to hunt for submarines.

"The Russian missile exploded inside the hangar. The fuel ignited, and the ready torpedoes exploded. The helicopters exploded. The fire spread into the ship. The crew couldn't put the fires out. The stern of the destroyer was ripped off when the fires reached the ship's fuel tanks that had that very morning been filled. The captain ordered the crew to abandon ship. The captain decided to go down with his ship. The captain used the 1MC to proudly say the pledge of allegiance as the ship slid under the waves. Only 100 managed to escape the burning and sinking destroyer. Some who were lucky to escape the sinking ship were sucked down with it as the ship sunk."

I didn't know what to say. I was shocked and felt sorry for those who died. "What was your mission?"

"We were part of the protection screen for the USS Nimitz, one of the Navy's nuclear-powered carriers. It had a crew of 5000 people and 75 planes. The Nimitz was hit by a weapon we didn't know the Russians had, a nuclear-armed wake-follower torpedo. The torpedoes followed the wake of the carrier, and when they got close, they exploded their 5 kiloton warheads. The two exploded within moments of each other. The 100,000-ton ship literally disappeared in the two mushroom clouds. The entire crew died with the carrier."

I whispered the one question I needed to know. I leaned toward the Lt.

Commander, Kevin Stark, "Commander, can I ask you a question?"

"Sure, what's on your mind?"

"Do you know who fired first?" I figured he knew more than us ground pounders. We didn't know anything. He had access to whatever intelligence that the Navy had before he lost his ship.

Commander Stark sat across from me, "Major, or should I call you general?"

"Major is fine, I was only frocked to BG so they had someone to blame. Who started this cluster?"

"In a manner, we did when NATO sent troops into Ukraine. Sending weapons was something, but when we directly entered the war, we became enemies of Russia. First, we sent weapons, then our president visited Ukraine while their president said he was going to use the tanks we were giving him to go all the way to Red Square. When the Ukrainians gave a poor showing in our tanks and Poland got hit, NATO decided for you guys to man the tanks and give Putin a bloody nose. I understand you guys did that and more."

I nodded, "We did, and I'm proud of how we performed, all the way up to when Putin decided to raise the odds. He responded by hitting our four field headquarters with tactical nukes. The next use of nukes struck the Russian troops. We were confused about who planted the nuke mines. The Russians, of course, thought NATO was behind it. NATO swore they had nothing to do with it. We said Putin hit his own troops as an excuse to expand the war. There were many in the Pentagon who thought Ukraine might have assembled the mines, but the Chairman of the Joint Chiefs dismissed that line of thought. He went with and advised it was a Russian false flag event.

"Threats were hurled back and forth. Every nuke-armed country placed their nukes on hot standby. We learned that some countries we suspected had nukes did in fact, have them."

Commander Stark asked, "Can you name a few?"

"How about Japan?"

"Really? Japan?"

"Not only did Japan out of the closet and tell the world she possessed nukes, they also announced their fighters could carry them and they had long range missiles that would enable them to strike China and/or Russia."

"Long-range missiles? Where did they come from?"

"They mounted a longer booster stage on standard anti-air missiles. They also worked with Israel on extending the range of their Jericho missiles. They can launch them from trains or trucks. The missiles were designed to be mobile."

"They're the last country I expected to have nukes."

"They decided as being the only country to have to suffer being attacked by two of them, they were going to ensure that if anyone, China, ever made noises of using nukes they'd be prepared to respond in kind. They also turned their subways and train tunnels into shelters."

I sat back, amazed, "Any other one pop up with a similar announcement?"

Stark nodded, "Yup, South Korea. The scuttlebutt was that we helped them build their bombs to face down the North. The real surprise was Saudi Arabia, and guess who helped them."

I nodded, "I can answer that one in one note, it has to be Israel. While they were playing patty cakes with China and Iran, they were building nukes with Israel's help so they'd have an ace in the hole if Iran ever got out of control."

I nodded and smiled, "Holy shit, it sounds like everyone came to this party dressed in their best."

"That's a hot understatement. Once the cat was out of the bag, the world paused to digest what they'd just learned. I can guess Putin wasn't very pleased with everyone having nukes and Russia being in range of some of those new ones."

I told Stark what I knew, I didn't care that the report had been marked Secret. Who was anyone going to tell while we were on this tub and who'd care right about now? "Of course, Putin threatened to destroy every member of NATO. NATO responded by saying that America and the UK would destroy Russia if they used another nuke. No one was sure what France would do. They had been in NATO and out, then back in as it suited them. This childish BS went back and forth until both sides were able to confirm the source of the enriched uranium. We blamed Russia for setting the nuclear mines as a way of getting rid of his C troops and blame us. This would give him an excuse to expand the war on his terms while making us the bad guys. Putin blamed us for stealing the uranium and using it to place the blame on Russia while killing thousands of Russians. We, by that, I mean America, went to the UN to demand they create a force to disarm Russia of her nuclear weapons. Of course, Russia vetoed the motion."

Stark asked, "Why would we go to the UN when we knew Russia could veto it? It seems to me a giant waste of time and resources."

I smiled, "Of course, it was. The use of nukes scared the administration since it would destroy the environment. They couldn't claim that man, and fossil fuels were the largest threat to the planet and then use environment-destroying weapons. They wanted to force the UN to do the dirty job they didn't have the balls to handle."

Stark looked surprised, "Shit, that must have been a real cluster. Were any sane minds in the room?"

I laughed, "You'd have thought so, but then our brilliant military minds decided this was the perfect time to run a nuke drill...."

Stark shook his head. "Now the alert messages we were receiving make sense. Our captain didn't understand what was going on. He was running the crew crazy with all the drills. Given the risk of someone making a mistake and tossing nukes around like candy, I can't believe anyone could be that stupid."

I nodded, "You'd be surprised how stupid some people can be. They ordered the bomber fleet to hot take off, nose to tail. They flushed the missile boats that had returned to port after the Russians nuked our four commanders. No sooner had they returned, they were ordered back to sea, and if that wasn't enough, the DHS announced mass Civil Defense drills."

Stark looked like he'd seen a ghost, his face turned pale white. "Oh, for the love of Jesus, Putin saw the drills and thought we were preparing to strike him."

I looked at the dregs in my coffee cup, "You won the grand prize. That's what happened. To our benefit, the drill included loading real nukes on the bombers, so when the Russians launched, we were prepared. What the fools didn't do was warn the president who was caught in his PJs in the middle of the night when they decided Putin decided the only way to survive and win the war was to take our leaders out. It didn't matter much by that time. We were ready to strike. All of our forces were as ready as a cocked pistol. The Russians executed a decapitation strike, the White House received a direct strike that destroyed it and the President in the bunker. They also hit the Pentagon as the same time as the White House."

Stark looked surprised, "If the president was dead who gave the order to strike? The Pentagon was hit at the same time as the White House. I think I heard that Cheyenne followed quickly after the White House. Who the hell pulled the trigger?"

I nodded. "Remember, some smart flag officer in the Pentagon didn't trust the president. He'd issued the orders to prepare us for the war. He prepared for the decapitation strike. He knew in his gut it was how Russia would strike. Remember, in the Russian planning, they launched one missile that released a series of large nukes in the upper atmosphere to generate a massive EMP spike to destroy all of our electronics. We got lucky. One of the interceptors from Fort Greely took that missile down before it could release its four warheads. The Russians had planned on a decapitating strike to take out our leaders and cripple our sensors, preventing us from issuing the order for our counter-strike. The Russians realized their first missile had been intercepted, so they launched three more. This time the interceptors managed to hit only one, the surviving two launched eight warheads that destroyed most of our electronics. Our military was prepared for the EMP, the general population wasn't."

Stark nodded, "I know our SM3 missiles could knock down medium-range missiles, but I didn't know those land-based anti-missile missiles really worked. We were one of the destroyers equipped with the SM3s. We used to laugh that they could have saved a ton of money by installing a larger booster on our SM3s and used them to knock down incoming missiles. The report I read in training for the SM3s said the ground-based interceptors weren't as accurate as our ship-based missiles, and we might get tasked to back them up."

I picked up on what Stark had said, "To a degree, they worked. Their largest weakness was we only had a small number of them. We were launching two or three at each incoming missile. We quickly realized we were playing a losing game."

"Tell me about it. We had the same situation with our destroyers, we only had a small number of interceptors. We couldn't reload at sea. The Russians kept track of the number of missiles we launched, and their first wave were missiles and drones that were designed to overwhelm our defenses. Some of those missiles didn't have warheads. They were loaded with chaff to blind our radars. They watched as we used up our missiles, then the next wave arrived right behind the first. Those missiles had jammers and a warhead. Those jammers took us by surprise. We lost the entire strike group and over 8,000 people due that trick. A trick similar to one Tom Clancy wrote about back in the 80s."

"I wonder if that's how they learned about the trick."

Stark slowly nodded, his eyes told me how hurt he was by the loss of so many shipmates. "I was able to read the intel right before my destroyer was struck and went down. The captain had downloaded it and handed it to me when we felt the ship shake from the first torpedoes. He told me to keep the report with me. He told me one day it might make an interesting book.

"Getting back to your question. I don't know who actually issued the order, but I can tell you the order originated from Cheyenne moments before it was destroyed. We also received the order from a TACAMO that said they got the order from the Mountain. Funny, now that you mention it, the planes never said who in the mountain issued the order. The TACAMO planes gave the go message to all of the Navy assets."

"A what?" I thought I knew all of the military's lingo, this was a new one to me.

"TACAMO. It stands for Take Charge And Move Out. They trail a long thin wire that sends a coded message to the missile boats. They also radio the DEFCON 1 order to all of our surface ships. Our carrier responded to the order by arming their attack birds with nukes. The admiral copied the message to all of the ships in the strike fleet, so we knew what was going on."

"I thought Bush one ordered the removal of nukes from the fleet."

"He did. A couple of weeks before the Russians began tossing nukes around, one of the president's aides handed him a stack of executive orders to sign. One of the EOs he signed was to rearm the Navy with nukes. The rumor is he had no idea what he was signing. It was just another in a stack of folders he was told to sign. One of the orders he signed ordered the Tridents to be rearmed with 10 warheads, so a typical Ohio class that carried 24 missiles now carried 240 warheads in their launch silos. Remember saying a smart officer in the Pentagon saw what Putin was up to? I have to assume he got the aide to draft the EO for the president to sign."

"That makes sense. I wonder who had the balls. He or she had to have known they weren't going to survive the first strike. How many missile boats did we have?"

Stark looked up as he was trying to remember, "Before the war, we had fourteen. One was being refueled so that left us with thirteen deployed. Those thirteen carried a total of 3,120 warheads, each was either 335 or 475 kilotons, and they were deadly accurate. Russia considered them a first-strike missile. I heard a rumor that they loaded the 14th while she was in dry dock, and her captain launched the missiles and ordered the crew to run as far and fast as possible."

"Why the different warheads?"

"The 475s were new, Obama stopped the updating of the older ones, so we made do with what we had. Still a lot better than the 12 kilotons we dropped on Japan."

"I'll say. Don't you wonder who the officers with balls was? The one issued the orders to prepare us for the, war and the other who issued the launch order."

Before Stark could say something more, a young captain pushed his way into the officers' mess. He stood on a chair, his eyes were glazed, he looked around the room. Many of us ignored him until he began screaming. "Listen to me, you fools. This wasn't the start of and end of the Third World War, this was the beginning of the end. Our Lord in Heaven has spoken to me. He had ordered me to tell all of you about Matthew, he spoke of these times thousands of years ago. Listen to the words of Matthew as he deemed they be written in the Bible is the word of God.

"You will hear of wars and rumors of wars but see to it that you are not alarmed. Such things must happen, but the end is still to come. Nation will rise against nation, and kingdom against kingdom. There will be famines and earthquakes in various places. All these are the beginning of birth pains.

"Then you will be handed over to be persecuted and put to death, and you will be hated by all nations because of me. At that time, many will turn away from the faith and will betray and hate each other, and many false prophets will appear and deceive many people. Because of the increase of wickedness, the love of most will grow cold, but the one who stands firm to the end will be saved. Don't you see how clearly his words ring today? We are living in the end times and will live to see the return of the Son and live forever in peace and safety. We might have to suffer some pain for the joys to come.

"I come to you to tell you to repent your sins while there is still time. Get on your knees and tell God you are a sinner and want to repent. Tell the Almighty that you accept His Son who died on the cross to cleanse you of your sins. Once you have repented, and I mean with all of your heart, you will be given a seat at the Son's table.

"Pray with me. Come outside to the flight deck with me. We will pray together, and we will share the peace the Son is bringing. He is bringing a thousand years of peace."

I looked for Stark, but he was gone. Someone I didn't know, someone without a name patch leaned and whispered to me, "That nut has been preaching the same drivel every day. You can set your watch by the time he gets up and begins yelling the same story. I don't know how you've missed it."

"Why doesn't the ship's security stop him?"

"He's not hurting anyone, and the captain thinks he might be helping some who are suffering. The captain said he believed there were many on this ship who were suffering. The ship lost its chaplain, so the captain lets him wander the ship tending to those who need that kind of help."

I could hear his words echoing through the halls of the ship. "He spends his day going to room to room telling everyone we're at the end of times?"

"Yup. The word is he doesn't sleep."

"How the hell could he go without sleep?"

"I can't answer that. Has he gotten to you? If it has, there is a group that meets with him every night at 1900 hours."

"Where do they meet?"

"On the hangar deck, near the bow."

After he was done with his preaching, he pointed at me. He said something so low I couldn't hear it. Other officers in the mess were whispering about me. I didn't care what they called me. I was brought up in the church. I remember the fiery sermons the priest used to almost scream at us every Sunday. The captain who was quoting Matthew reminded me of my childhood priest. I remembered the sermons when he said God would bring forth the end of times by sending fire from the skies. Is that what happened in the past month? God promised he wouldn't flood the earth again, but he didn't say he wouldn't use fire which is what got us. Missiles with their nuclear warheads falling from the sky.

The 1MC squawked to get our attention, "This is the captain, we will be arriving stateside in 36 hours. A Coast Guard and or a Navy Frigate will check us out before we'll be allowed in the harbor. Remember, we're all on the same side. They have a job to do as you did yours. Once we dock, you'll be given your new orders. I may not have the opportunity to address you again. I want to wish all of you the best."

Our orders? I wonder how many will hang around. I bet most will run the moment we tied up. I looked around wondering where did Stark go? He didn't answer my question, or he was afraid to answer it.

Chapter 9

I found a nice quiet place to sit by myself and do some thinking about the few members of my family. I know my cousins who lived near Cape Hatteras, and the couple that lived in northern New Jersey were most probably gone. That only left one in South Florida that I'd guess didn't make it. For some reason, Miami seemed to be a juicy target for the Russians, as they hit it three times. That left my uncle and cousins in eastern Tennessee. I can't remember how close they were to Oak Ridge, which I'm sure was a target. If they all died, then my line would end with me. I never married. I didn't want to go to war worried about my wife getting the call in the middle of the night.

I kind of knew those that lived along the coast from Charlotte, South Carolina, to Boston would have died from the Russian's monster nuclear torpedo that exploded underwater. It carried the mission it was designed for. It caused a gigantic tidal wave that carried radioactive water up to fifty miles inland. In one fell swoop, they managed to destroy all of our bases and our eastern coastal cities that, included Charlotte and Norfolk, which was the world's largest naval base. The cities of Philadelphia, Newark, New York, and Groton, which was the location of our largest submarine base, and Boston were all destroyed. I heard some experts question if the submarine-launched missiles or the radioactive tidal wave did more damage to Washington, D.C. I remembered the Captain's map, the entire east coast was dark from fallout or, as I've now learned, from the nuclear torpedo that spread death along our coasts.

Unlike defenses against missiles, there wasn't any defense against a torpedo. The launching submarine was hundreds of miles from our coast when it launched the giant torpedo. The weapon was a true fire and forget. I guess, but I don't know for a fact, they used at least one against our west coast too. I intend to find out the facts when I get off this tub.

I'd heard a rumor in the weather center of the ship that the torpedo may have also screwed with the Gulf Stream. If that was true, they might have dealt the UK and Europe the cruelest blow. The warm waters of the Gulf Stream kept the UK and most of Europe from being turned into a frozen landmass. Putin was a believer in destroying the west and the modern era so the Russian people would emerge to rule the remains. I believe Putin thought if he knocked out the President and the Pentagon, we wouldn't be able to respond before his missiles destroyed our bases and our silo-based Minutemen ICBMs, knocking two of the legs of our nuclear triad down. Shame on them, that's not what happened. We'd had a decapitation strike war plan for decades. Launch authority moved from person to person, so we didn't lose a minute in retaliation.

Putin and his advisors either forgot, or it was a secret we actually managed to keep. With all of the spies in D.C. it's a wonder we were able to keep anything a secret. As soon as the Russian nukes hit our command areas in Ukraine, a very astute senior officer in the Pentagon issued the orders to return nuclear weapons to our ships and to return to flying our bombers, loaded with nukes around the clock. The commanding general of the Air Force brought back the Cold War plan of sending bombers and refueling planes to what were called Fail-Safe locations. These are areas outside of Russia's airspace. The bombers could launch their long-range cruise missiles from these locations without having to even enter Russia's air space. The refueling planes would fill the tanker's fuel tanks just before they dove for their low-altitude bombing runs. The crews hoped their cruise missiles and the sub and land-based missiles destroyed the Russian air defense so they could strike their targets and get home alive.

The B-2 and B-21 bombers flew a different flight plan. They wanted to strike at night and from a higher altitude than the B-52s. I later learned that the president never knew what was happening right under his nose. He would have most likely pooped his pants had he known we were flying nuclear-armed planes so close to Russian airspace.

The navy quickly filled their underway replenishment ships with nukes that were delivered to the fleets at sea. They also delivered Marines to guard the nukes as was the case in the cold-war. The Trident Submarine base at Kingsport, Georgia, had been tasked to swap the conventional warheads in each of the 154 Tomahawks that filled the missile containers in the four SSGN submarines with nuclear warheads. While that was happening, the president said we wouldn't accept the use of nuclear weapons in Ukraine. He said he was conferring with the leaders of NATO on what our response should be. The US Military didn't wait for NATO's political leaders, they prepared for all-out nuclear war.

The CIA leaked to their counterparts in Russia that the American military was prepared to wage a full nuclear war. The Russians didn't believe the American president would have the guts to order a nuclear strike, they also didn't believe the story the CIA had told them that the military had acted without the president's knowledge of arming the fleet and air force with nuclear weapons and America was now prepared to respond with over 5,000 nuclear weapons. Putin ordered his military not to believe the fake news from the American CIA and to prepare to go ahead with their strike plan. When the CIA leaks didn't get the desired results, the Chairman of the Joint Staffs attempted to call his counterpart in Russia to whisper the same information. His counterpart refused his call.

The same officer in the Pentagon who had secretly issued the arm orders knew the Chairman was a risk and an officer he didn't trust. A few clandestine meetings and the Chairman's car was struck by a tractor-trailer. The Chairman's driver had been tipped off. He stopped at a red light, opened his door and ran for his life. The Chairman shouted what was going on, and then bam the truck crushed the limo he was sitting in. Almost no one in the middle ranks shed a tear. Those who couldn't be trusted quickly learned they had three options, get on the horse, resign or suffer the same fate as the Chairman. Some attempted to go to the press, they never made it home. In the end, the Pentagon worked around the clock cutting red tape and preparing the military for war. Had the war not happened a handful of flag rank officers would have been put against a wall and shot for treason. With the White House, Pentagon and Cheyenne gone, no one who knew was around to blow the whistle.

In the cold war the Air Force flew nuclear command planes they code named Looking Glass. The commanding general had the authority to issue the launch codes if the president was killed. I guess they quietly flew the Looking Glass planes and gave the commanding flag officer the launch computer and launch codes. I wondered who else had the launch computers and was given the authority to issue the launch codes. With the Pentagon and Cheyenne gone, I'm not sure we'll ever know who else they had trusted.

I was lost in my thoughts while I began making a list of who else I thought would have been given a computer. I didn't pay much attention to the various announcements from the 1MC. That was until Neal stood over me, "Hey, do you know the captain's looking for you?"

"Huh? What's he want with me?"

"I think that's why he wants you to report to his cabin. He's announced it three times. I bet he's sent the ship's police to search for you."

I slowly got up and looked around, sure enough, a dog and his handler were coming towards us. I bet they brought the dog to my bunk to set a smell of me, then the dog picked up my scent and brought his handler to me.

"The captain has ordered us to locate you and escort you to his cabin."

The captain's cabin was much smaller than I expected. He had a small desk, his bunk, a closet, and a head. He pointed to a chair across from him. He took me by surprise when he stood up and saluted me. I knew I was in deep shit when he did that. "Captain, I'm a major, you're a naval captain, which means you're a full colonel, and from where I'm from a colonel outranks a major."

The captain smiled and handed me a fax. I read it and shook my head. I was frocked as a BG to organize what was left of the division, and since I was writing the battle plans, the Pentagon decided I would be listened to if I had ranked over the battalion commanders. In my heart, I'm really a major. "Captain..."

"General, I suggest you read the signature on the fax. It looks like the President's to me."

"He can't have promoted me to Lt. General from being a major."

"There aren't many flag officers left. Many died in Washington. Others died when their bases were nuked. The President and his staff reviewed the background of every existing flag officer. Based on your performance in Ukraine, they decided on you to carry out the orders I'm supposed to hand you. You aren't being promoted to Lt. General from Major, you're being promoted from Brigadier General to Lt. General, congratulations."

"No, no. They've got the wrong guy. I'm no general officer."

"This says you are, and until they locate someone of a higher rank in any service you're in charge. So general, what are your orders."

I was shocked and dumbfounded, "Oh, my God. I can't imagine what he wants of me. Wait, you say it's from the president?"

"Check the signature on the bottom of the fax."

"Wait, I thought all the members of Congress and the president's cabinet died in Washington."

"I thought so too. I asked him to explain how he survived. He told me he was on a plane from California when Washington got hit. His plane suffered a catastrophic failure when the EMP bombs exploded. They managed to glide without engine power into the Fort Huachuca Missile Range Army Base in Otero, NM. The pilot managed to land on the sand without any injuries. Some of the engineers who were based on the range saw the plane crash land. They rushed to provide support. They were surprised when the crew and passengers deplaned, and they saw the Speaker of the House and two Secret Service agents on board.

"They asked the Speaker if he knew about the attacks, he said he assumed we were under attack by someone due to the bright flashes in the sky and the plane's loss of power. The speaker asked about Washington. He was told the base had lost communication with anyone on the east coast, no one answered, and even their secure fiber network was dead.

"The Secret Service asked if the base had a judge, they were told there was one in the community around ten miles away. The engineers realized why they were asking. An Army HUMVEE was sent to bring the judge to the base to administer the oath of office to the Speaker. An hour later, we had a new president."

"Where is the president now?"

"He had planned to go to Cheyenne when he learned it was destroyed. I understand he's still at Fort Huachuca until the Secret Service and Military Police can figure out a secure place to house him. The test area is huge in size. It's the country's largest military facility. The Secret Service turned the commanding general's quarters into a new White House, and they built a fence around it. I know from a friend who was based there for a year that they have a few platoons of military police to patrol the borders to make sure no unauthorized people entered the base. The president called for all local members to report to the base."

I briefly remembered the base from a month I spent watching new anti-armor missiles being tested. "Captain, do you know what he wants from me?"

"Since I had to decode his orders for you, I do know what he wants, and all I can say is better you than me." He handed me a sealed envelope bordered in red with a large TOP SECRET stamped on it with the address, "For the Eyes of General Morton only."

I looked at the captain. "Captain, I have no new orders for you. Please follow the last ones you received."

"Yes, sir. Thank you, sir."

I stood dumbfounded. I looked at the small box in the captain's hands. He held a box with three shiny silver stars. He said, "I checked, we don't have the patch with three stars in the ship's store, but we did have the stars in stock. General, may I be the first to congratulate you on your promotion? He jumped to attention and saluted me. I shook my head. I gave him a small return salute. "Please sit, I mean, as you were.

"If I remember correctly, we're docking at Mayport, which is a long way from Fort Huachuca. How do they expect me to get there? Hitch? Do know if the interstates have been cleared from here to there?"

"I wouldn't worry about the interstates. The president sent a plane for you. Turns out there were a lot of planes at Fort Huachuca. Most were in secure hangars when the bombs went off. You lucked out, I understand he sent a G-550 Gulfstream for you. The plane has a range of 6,750 miles, so you'll have no problem making it to Fort Huachuca without refueling. You'll be taking two other passengers. One is an FBI special agent tasked with your protection. There aren't any Secret Service agents at Mayport. Normally you'd supply your own security, but given the short time you've been a general, and you don't even have a chief of staff, it was decided to ask the FBI to keep an eye on you. Your other passenger is from naval intelligence, who will brief you on the flight."

"Can I appoint anyone I want as my chief of staff?"

"Of course, according to this fax, you're in charge of the US Military. Do you have someone in mind?"

"I do."

Fifteen minutes later, Neal was escorted into the Captain's cabin. His eyes went wide when he saw the three silver stars on my collar. "Sir!" He snapped to attention. "May I ask the general a question?"

"Permission granted." Shit. I was even starting to sound like a general.

"Sir, I thought we changed from wearing our ranks on our collars to patches. Is this for real?"

The captain smiled, "Captain, it is for real. We didn't have any three-star patches, but we did locate one set of pins. It's not every day I get to pin three stars on someone."

"Old friend, I have some good and bad news for you…"

"No way. I'm turning down any promotion you offer me to be your CoS. I'm leaving the service as soon as we dock and finding a nice little place to call home."

"Captain," I smiled, more of a leer, "According to an executive order signed by the new president, I am in charge of the US military, and he canceled all leaves and all retirements so congratulations, you're now a Lt. Colonel and my CoS."

"Tom, I mean, sir, please don't do this to me."

"I already did. Captain, could you please inform Mayport there will be another passenger to accompany me to Fort Huachuca? I'd also like to see if the two of us can get a fresh uniform. These are a little worse for wear, and I don't think we're going to have time to get them laundered."

"Not a problem. Why don't the two of you clean up, I'll have an aide bring you fresh uniforms. General, I believe you should start wearing your name and the US Army tags so people know who you are and deck apes don't pick fights with you. I'd hate to report we lost another enlisted due to the general shooting them with a concealed handgun, one that's forbidden on the ship."

"Yes, sir."

"Remember, I call you sir. You address me as captain or anything you'd like. In the Navy, a three-star flag officer is a Vice Admiral. You outrank me by three grades."

"Captain, since I outrank you by three grades, can't I make the rules about carrying concealed weapons?"

"Sir, my ship isn't going to be turned into the wild west. You may have the stars, but this is still my ship. I will make sure the security platoon assigns some people to be your protection detail while you're on my ship."

"Thank you."

The captain held out his hand, "Sir, the small pistol I know you're still carrying on your person. I know you picked the pocket of my police officer. He went to turn it in and had to report he'd lost it someplace on the ship. I knew then that you still had it."

I patted my uniform, "These uniforms have a lot of pockets and space. Here it is." I handed it to the captain who nodded at me.

"General, I can assure you, you are safe on my ship. I don't want to have to face the president and tell him his new Chairman of the Joint Chiefs was murdered on my ship. I've ordered the ship's police to cover you around the clock."

"Captain, thank you. I'm sure I'm in good hands." Neal smiled, he knew I most likely had at least one other gun hidden.

Neal and I were shown to an empty cabin that I was going to use as my office until we docked at Mayport. I handed Neal the envelope with my orders. "Please read, and then we can discuss what the president wants from me, now us."

Neal nodded, "Tom..."

"You can use my first name when we're alone, but never when we're in public."

Neal began reading the orders that were organized more like a report with a list of requests. Neal looked across the small desk at me, "He doesn't want much does he? Does he know we don't have any infrastructure? No comms, no idea of the rails or roads. A quarter of the country has so much junk in the atmosphere our planes can't fly, and he wants your plan on how to not only rebuild but also arrange the surviving military to protect us from anything the few surviving Russians try or the Chinese who have been very quiet lately."

"Did you read the lines on pages three and four that he wants us to act like Lewis and Clark and recon the cities and waterways?"

"Why not send a drone?"

"He wants boots on the ground. He asked me to find a Spec Four ODA team to perform the recon. Then on page six, he wants a plan for action if the Chinese get rowdy. Did you know when we and the Russians were dancing, the Chinese took Taiwan?"

Neal looked surprised, "When did they invade?"

"Hours after the Ukrainians set off their nuclear mines. The Taiwanese managed to hold the Chinese off for days. The PRC knew we'd be focused on Ukraine and wouldn't bat an eye at anything that happened in the South China Sea. They were right. Tens of thousands died. The PRC hit the island with hundreds of missiles, Taiwan struck the mainland with rockets, and their F-16s dropped load after load on the PLANAVY bases. They also caught their invasion in the straits. They managed to sink over 60% of the invasion fleet. They used thousands of suicide drones. We'll have lots of time to discuss the situation in the Pacific, right now, we should review these orders and figure out how we can carry them out."

"Boss, you need a staff. Can I recruit some people from the boat?"

"Might as well. You're right, I do need a staff, and this tub is filled with experienced officers. Let me know whom you recommend."

"I'll have a list for you before we dock."

Neal left to start the work the president asked of us. I sat with my notebook thinking of how we can perform the recon we were asked to perform. We're going to need all of the overhead images we can get our hands on. I'm also going to need radiation readings for every city and every ground zero. I don't want to send anyone into a situation where they might get sick from lingering radiation.

Chapter 10

When Neal and I left the USS Wasp, every member of the military snapped to attention and saluted us. I put my hand up to my brow and held the salute until we were escorted to an armored LAV that took us to the airport, where our plane waited. A Naval intelligence officer, a young woman wearing the rank tab of two bars, met us there. I returned her salute and remembered in the Navy, the two bars meant she was called a Lieutenant, while in the Army, Marines and Air Force would be called a captain. Her name tag was Davis. "Lieutenant Davis, I assume you're here to brief us on the war and the current situation of the war and the country."

"Yes, sir. I have a secure tablet for you and some maps we compiled from our overhead birds, and we sent our three Auroras to photograph our country."

I looked at Neal, who shrugged his shoulders. "Excuse me, Lieutenant, what's an Aurora?"

"Sir, I'm sorry. I forgot you spent your carrier in the Army. The Aurora is the replacement for the SR-71. The plane is classified Top Secret. It's the world's fastest and highest-flying plane. No surface-to-air missile can reach it, nor can any fighter. It's stealthy, fast, and can fly above 90,000 feet."

"How do the engines run at 90,000 feet? There's not enough oxygen up there."

"The plane's normal jet engines take the plane to 50,000 feet and Mach 3, then the inlet air ramps change shape so the air is rammed into the engines. The engines become SCRAMJETs that powers the plane to Mach 6 and allows it to fly close to 100,000 feet. It is a manned missile. It has a crew of two, the pilot and a mission specialist who mans the cameras and sensors. We've been flying the SR-72 for five years."

"We have images of our cities and bases?"

"Sir, why don't you get comfortable on the plane. We have a long flight, and I have a lot of information to brief you on. The president wants you brought up to date on everything we know. Sir, one issue is that my orders are to brief you. I don't know who the colonel is. He's not on my list."

"He's my Chief of Staff. I promoted him to colonel and made him my CoS when we were on the ship. I sent the information to Fort Huachuca."

"Sir, would you mind while I confirm with Fort Huachuca?"

"Not at all. If he's not cleared for the flight, then neither am I."

"Sir, my orders come directly from the president."

"So do mine. He appointed me the defacto commander of the US Military, which means I have the authority to promote or demote anyone I please and to appoint my own CoS."

"Sir, I was told a CoS was waiting for you at Fort Huachuca..."

"I have no such information, and as I've said, if the colonel isn't cleared for the flight, neither am I. I'll contact the president and make my case which will include you serving time on a recovery mission to Washington."

Davis' tablet pinged, "Sir, the colonel has been cleared as he is now carried as your aide-de-camp. I'll arrange for his badge and Aiguillette when we reach Fort Huachuca. Sir, I have your TS/SCI card. The colonels will be waiting for us when we land."

"Colonel, am I correct that you've never been an Aide-de-Camp before?"

"That's correct Are there any specific rules I need to know?"

"Colonel, the most important rule is to remember you exist to make the general's life easier, and you exist to make him look good. You don't sell favors or play games with other officers. I know the two are close, but remember, do not use that relationship to sway the general to a decision that isn't for the best of America. Your boss is number one behind the CIC, so don't plan any pranks. They'll look bad on the general and on the president for selecting him. Am I clear?"

I saw Neal nod. "Colonel, I want to hear the words from your mouth."

Neal looked at me, I nodded my head back at him. "I promise to always protect the general and the president. I'll have their backs even if it means mine."

"Excellent. Colonel, welcome to the party."

Neal smiled. He looked at Davis, "Did I miss a party? I always like a good party."

"Colonel, the party you and the general will be attending for the next few years is the reconstruction and defense of the country."

Neal slowly nodded his head. "I understand. No victory parades for us."

"At least not yet. The president has a lot of confidence in the general, and by association, you. Colonel, don't let either of them or the country down."

"I promise to do the best I can do."

"Excellent." We were interrupted by the sound of the plane's engines spooling up, and just like that, we were in the air. There were the three of us and an Air Force master sergeant who acted as our flight attendant. He was also part of our security team. I learned we'd pick up a full-time security team when we landed. I waited till our coffee was served, then I looked at Davis, "We're in the air, we're alone except for the sergeant. I think I'm ready to listen to your update."

"Sir, if you'll place your finger on the fingerprint pad, I will walk you through the timeline of the Third World War."

"Here goes nothing." The tablet came to life and asked me to look into the camera so it could check my face against the database so the tablet would know I was the authorized user.

"Sir, if I can call your attention to the file labeled timeline. I'll walk you through the information. Much of it you may also know. Some of the events you lived through and may be able to add details we're missing."

I looked at Neal, who was visibly sweating. He had been much closer to some of the nukes I had been. I know he was suffering from radiation poisoning. I don't think he knew that I knew. I was hoping that doctors at the base could do something for him. He was my best and maybe my only surviving friend.

I tapped the icon on my tablet. "I opened the icon, I think I know how the start of this mess happened. I was there."

"Do you remember what happened when the Ukrainians attacked the Russian T-90 and T-14 tanks with their Centurion tanks?"

"Sure, the Ukrainians got their asses kicked. They drove into a classic ambush. It's one thing to have modern equipment. It's another to know how to use the equipment. The Russians knew the Ukrainians would be cocksure with their new toys and wouldn't be experts with them yet. The Centurions may have been a better tank, the Ukrainians didn't have the training to fight them at the level the Russians had. The Ukrainians lost most of their new toys."

"Do you know what happened next?"

"Yes. Putin laughed and told NATO if we continued to send tanks to Ukraine, then he'd be happy to return the burnt carcasses of our tanks to us while his superior Russian tanks rolled up the rest of Ukraine. Putin told NATO if they didn't stop shipping modern tanks, he would strike at their assembly locations, even if that meant striking a location in a NATO country.

"NATO's leaders debated what to do for weeks. Our Secretary of Defense, who was opposed to sending tanks to Ukraine, told the NATO military officers the Ukrainians not only weren't well trained enough to use the modern tanks we had promised them, but they needed years of training to not only fight with the tanks, but they needed to know how to maintain them. Modern tanks were very complex vehicles and needed constant care, something the Ukrainians weren't able to pull off. We told the NATO military leaders that without the proper training, the Ukrainians were most likely going to lose the battle against the Russian tanks, and they'd end up losing the war.

"That speech to the NATO military leaders was the single argument that led NATO to come to the conclusion that the only way to win the war and destroy Russia's military was to send NATO troops to fight the battles in our equipment. Remember, our goal was to declaw the Russian Bear so they couldn't pose a threat to anyone for a very long time."

"That's the same time that Russia struck Poland and they declared Article 5. Had the Poles not declared the 5 the world be a much different place."

Davis looked very darkly at me, "Sir, they were right to declare they'd been attacked, and they needed the other members of NATO to their aid."

"There had to have been a different way. The politicians should have realized how Putin would react. We played right into his hand. Their simple act led to the nuclear war that killed billions."

"Sir, when did you arrive in country?"

"We were mobilized within an hour of NATO's vote to honor Poland's request. I thought we had stepped on the Bear's toes, and the outcome of defeating Russia would be something much different than the Sec DoD thought. Putin had told the world he would defend Russia with every weapon in its arsenal, including the use of nuclear weapons. He told us what was coming, and we thought he was bluffing.

"The fools made their vote very public. So public that they pushed Putin into a corner. We never learned it's not a good idea to push bullies into a corner without giving them a way to get out of the corner and save face. We made Putin lose face. He knew his tanks didn't stand a chance against our tanks manned by our best. He had warned NATO of the consequences if we went ahead with our plans to send NATO troops to face Russian troops on the battlefield. Putin sent NATO a formal letter promising he would use every weapon in his armory if NATO sent troops into Ukraine.

"What did we do? We ignored his letter and went ahead with our deployments."

Davis said, "You're correct. Hindsight is always 20/20. We screwed up and now we have to rebuild."

I nodded, pleased that Davis understood how badly NATO had screwed up. "I know a few of the problems we faced. I learned some from prisoners we captured. When we were deploying, Putin was having his own problems. One of his elite tank brigades, the 155th lost over 5,000 personnel and was almost wiped out in January of '23. They were supposed to receive the new T-14 tank as a replacement for their T-90s, which were destroyed by the Javelins we gave the Ukrainians. They didn't receive any of the so-called advanced Armada tanks because they had been rushed through production and suffered from quality problems, so they were given 50-year-old T-62 tanks. The Russians were running out of modern weapons, thus their purchases from Iran and requests to China. There had even been rumors they had pulled T-54 tanks that had been produced in the 1950s.

"The Russians never threw any military equipment away. When it came to tanks, they had warehouses of them. They simply performed maintenance and updated the tanks before they were sent to the front. After receiving these relics of the Cold War, the 115th was ordered to drive through a famous Ukrainian minefield.

Their officers and soldiers refused. Can you imagine a Russian brigade committing mutiny fifty years ago? This should have been a large red flag, that Putin was so low on munitions, he was going to have to resort to using his nuclear arsenal. We were so blinded by our wanting to crush Putin that we missed all the signs.

"When Russia first invaded Ukraine, we missed our chance of suggesting a cease-fire. We had stopped the previous discussion, and our egos got in the way of logic. We promised the Ukrainians a blank check so they could hurt the Russians. We made a serious mistake. Putin sent us the message, and we ignored it."

Neal shook his head, "I find it hard to believe an entire Russian brigade mutinied. Fifty years ago, they would have been killed by their political officers. I'd heard they had a morale issue, but not that some of their units flatly refused their orders."

I smiled, thinking of the Russians facing significant mutinies. "I remember reading the intel reports, the Russians were also running out of smart weapons. If I remember correctly, they were buying drones and missiles from Iran. I bet Israel was happily watching Iran deplete the weapons Iran planned to use on them."

Davis nodded her head, "Israel was pleased Iran was quickly depleting their best weapons. They didn't like the idea of the weapons being used against NATO, so the MOSSAD agents struck and destroyed a number of factories and weapons storage sites. They torched the factories, and in the process, they killed a number of Iran's best weapons scientists. Russia continued to rely on Iranian smart weapons all of 2023. The Russian spring offensive was delayed due to a shortage of weapons. Some units reported a shortage of basic ammo. Tank crews said they were sent to the front with their magazines only 75% full."

Neal smiled, "Most of the Russians we came into contact with didn't have the opportunity to fire more than one round before we capped them. Their turrets shot into the air like they had rocket engines shooting them into the sky. We could target and hit them before their shells could reach us. Ours hit their tanks, and their shells landed in the dirt hundreds of meters in front of our tanks. We'd heard that the Russians could fire on the move, but we didn't see it. Our tanks could and did. Our tanks communicated with each other, so no Russian tank was targeted by more than one of ours.

"Don't even get me started on air support. Once NATO opened the floodgates, we flew F-22 and F-35s over the battlefield. We owned the sky, then our two ground attack planes went to work. The A-10s killed tanks and their armored vehicles while the AC-130J Ghost Riders worked over their unarmored troops. The ACs were armed with 30mm and 105mm cannons. They also fired missiles and dropped bombs. The A-10s hit the second and third waves of Russian vehicles. Their fighters were no match for our fifth-generation planes. Our planes were able to shoot the Russians down before they even knew they were being targeted, and then it was all over. Our missiles were smart enough to know a plane from decoys or flares. We shot down every fighter they were foolish enough to send up against us. Once the threat of Russian fighters was ended, the ground attack planes mopped up any tanks and vehicles we missed, and let me tell you if we could see them, we killed them. We fought as we had trained. In fact, the training was harder than the actual battles, and the rules of the game were changed."

Davis asked, "Colonel, you were on the front lines, what happened? According to what you just said, we should have won, and bingo, the war would be over."

Neal got a stoic look on his face, "What happened? Putin let the genie out of the bottle again. We were winning. We could have pushed them across the border. I thought we should have continued to Moscow and arrested or shot Putin. Then in a series of blinding flashes, the war in Ukraine was over. I lost most of my people. Did you ever see a 70-ton tank knocked on its side? How about the paint on the tanks bubble and burn? Did you ever skin bubble and melt? My crews died doing their jobs."

The only sound in the cabin was that of the engines. I called a ten-minute break. I knew what was coming. Part of me didn't want to hear of the suffering of our people. People we had sworn to protect. We had failed them.

Davis must have realized what I was thinking, "General, you didn't fail the American public, the politicians did."

Chapter 11

Davis connected her laptop to a projector so both of us could follow her as she started discussing the timeline of the war, a timeline we both thought we knew. I did want to understand how the world as we knew it was destroyed in a few hours.

She saw that both of us were tense and angry, so she went slow and attempted not to hit on any of our tender spots. That lasted less than a minute. "General, I know you have first-hand experience with the Russian weapons that destroyed NATO's four command posts..."

"First-hand experience like I saw the flash that killed my general and his staff. Most of them were my friends. First-hand, like being ordered to return to ground zero to look for any survivors and determine if the general had died in the explosion. Do you know what a body looks like after they're caught under a nuke? Some are vaporized like a bad science fiction movie. Some are burned so badly that you have a hard time determining if they're human. Facial features are gone, toes and fingers are burned off. They look like charred meat that's been left on the grill too long.

"I couldn't find any dog tags. They had melted from the heat of the explosion. Forget teeth. I told Washington the general and his staff were gone. I counted the bodies that were tents when the nuke exploded and the six outside. The tents themselves were gone. They had been vaporized, everyone and everything in the general's camp were gone."

Davis looked confused, "General, what do you mean when you said they were gone, or I believe the word you used was vaporized? How could a body be vaporized? First-hand? Yeah, I had first-hand knowledge. The pentagon kept pushing me to confirm the general was dead. How do you identify one lump of charred meat from another? Yeah, I had first-hand knowledge. I have nightmares every night about what I saw and smelled."

I was angry. They had sent us a rookie with no knowledge of nuclear weapons to brief us on the nuclear war, "Lieutenant, do you know anything about how a nuclear bomb operates or what happens when one explodes?"

"Sir, I don't. I'm in intelligence. I was ordered to brief you, which is what I'm trying to do."

"Lieutenant, when a nuclear weapon explodes, it sends out a thermal pulse, that's heat to you. That pulse is hotter than the surface of the sun. Do you understand what I just said? It's why a nuclear weapon creates so many serious burn cases. If we add all of our burn centers in pre-war America and Europe together, they couldn't cope with the burn cases from one bomb. ONE, not the four the Russians used on NATO's field command centers. These were small nukes, not the city busters used when we and the Russians were tossing ICBMs across the pole at each other.

"Each explosion released a flash brighter than the sun. Thousands of civilians were blinded when they looked at the blasts. Anyone looking in the direction of the flash would have had their retinas burned. Some would be lucky enough to have some of their sight returned. Most who looked and you had to look at the flash would be permanently blind.

"They were burned when the thermal pulse hit them and set their homes and everything in them on fire, the pulse burned their clothing and their skin. and then there was the radiation.

"The explosion released radioactive atoms, think of them as invisible, micro bullets that traveled at the speed of light, which happens to be 186,000 miles per second. These radioactive bullets tore into the human body destroying bone marrow, organs and leaving behind a walking dead person who was going to die between an hour to a few days. The lucky ones were the ones caught under the fireball. They died instantly. The unlucky ones were the ones who survived the initial thermal and radiation. They were doomed to a very painful and slow death. Radiation poisoning is a slow, horrible way to die. There's no cure.

"The radiation kills the bone marrow, it kills the body's organs. Your teeth and hair fall out. You can't keep anything in your stomach. You'll be throwing up while you have diarrhea. It comes out both ends at the same time. You'll pray for death, then on the third or fourth day, you'll feel better. In reality, it's playing a game with you. The next day and the day after will be the worst. You'll have blood flowing from every orifice, and on the fourth or fifth day, you'll die.

"I forgot about the blast wave. The human body implodes with an external pressure of 5 psi, the bombs produced blast waves in the order of up to 50 psi. Buildings and bodies just blew apart."

Davis sat with her mouth hanging open. "I didn't know. How many died that way?" Her face was pale, and her hands shook.

I looked into her eyes, "In Ukraine? Everyone who lived in the blast or fallout zone of those initial four small weapons, which I'd estimate twenty to fifty thousand died. Once the tossing of nukes in Ukraine was over, I'd guess 95% of the people who were still in country died within the first ten days."

"What about Europe?" asked Davis.

"Millions and millions. I'd estimate that by the end of the first year, close to 95% of the population will have died. Many from radiation, starvation, lack of common drugs like insulin. Many will die due to exposure. There is a rumor that Russia's nuclear torpedo they exploded off our east coast screwed up the gulf stream. If that happened, then the UK and Europe are in for a very nasty winter with no food, very little shelter, and no fuel to generate heat."

She was a pale as freshly fallen snow, "Will it be that bad back home?"

"I'd wage we lost sixty to eighty million in the explosions and another hundred million from the fallout in the first month. We're also going to face the losses from starvation, lack of clean water, exposure, lack of drugs, fighting over limited resources, and lack of shelters. Then there are the cancers and other diseases that will sweep across the northern hemisphere. When the final numbers are tallied, if they ever are, I estimate we're going to lose up to 90% of our population."

Davis ran to the small toilet at the back of the plane and threw up. Neal and I refilled our coffee cups. Neal blew on his to cool it then he sipped his mug, "They must have stolen some navy coffee because is better than what they served us on base. I like the logos on the mugs. You need to get us some mugs like these."

I looked at him and smiled. "I think our intel puke, just puked."

Neal tried to hold in a laugh. I smiled at my own joke.

Neal smiled, "Oh, I get it. The big cheese is on board, so we get the good stuff. I think I may get to like this job."

"You better because I don't want to break in some young pup who's green behind his ears."

Neal pointed to the toilets, "Example number one."

I smiled and nodded. I called another ten-minute break so Davis could pull herself together. She sat next to Neal. She saw I was busy with messages, so she decided to talk to Neal, "How do you do it?"

"Do what?"

"Look at death every day without it affecting you?"

"Don't get us wrong. It affects us. It hits us very hard. Seeing our people die. Holding a young soldier dying in your arms gives you nightmares. The first couple are very hard, and then you steel yourself. You have to build a cage around your soul so you can handle what you see on the battlefield. Friends you made, some for ten or twenty years, dying in front of you, and you are helpless to do anything. Believe us, we feel it. We carry each of those deaths around our necks. They're always there. Sometimes they talk to us. Other times they're just ghosts."

"You believe in ghosts?"

"Do this job long enough, and you'll believe too."

Davis began to shake. Neal hugged her to calm her. She smiled and replied, "Thank you. Be careful, doing that a few times could lead to other activities. Some we shouldn't get caught doing on this plane."

Neal hugged Davis again, "There's tonight after we land."

Davis smiled, "There's always tonight. Do you think the general will need my services after we land?"

"Only to help us to our offices, and where we're going to live while we're here."

"What do you mean, while we're here? That sounds like you're not planning on being on base for a long time."

"We're not. Part of our assignment is to scout the country to see how bad the damage is."

"You just explained what happens from a nuclear burst. Are you crazy going into what you call ground zero? Why?"

"Because those are our orders. We can't help people who, for some reason or other, don't want to be found. We have to know or have a good estimate of how many of us survived. Our government is based on representing people. The House is divided by the states' population. Some states may have lost so many people their number of representatives will drop to one."

"I understand that, but is safe for people to live in their homes? Won't they get infected by the fallout?"

Neal leaned over and whispered in Davis' right ear. "Radiation is not contagious, it's not a disease you catch. I already have a case of radiation poisoning. I don't want anyone to know, especially the general."

"Would you like to make a small wager on it?" Asked Davis, who wanted to make it simpler for Neal.

"What makes you so sure he knows?"

"I guessed it as soon as the general explained what happened when a nuke explodes. I saw the blood around your teeth. You try to hide it by not opening your mouth in a way that no one can see your teeth. A couple of times, you slipped, and I saw them. The general misses nothing. He knows, but he figures you'll tell him when you're ready. It's one of the reasons he appointed you his aide-de-camp. You're friends, I bet very close friends, so he wants to protect you and keep you around as long as possible. As his aide, he can make sure you receive the best medical care we can provide."

Neal slowly nodded his head, "We are close. I'd consider him my best friend, and I'm sure he feels the same about me. I thought he was killed when the command center was taken out, and I know he thought I was killed when Putin used nukes on us. We literally bumped into each other on the ship. Do you know he spent most of the trip incognito on the deck wearing a blouse without a name, service, or rank on it? He liked the sea air, and he didn't want to be bothered. He was mourning for the millions who'd died or will die."

"He didn't kill them."

"You don't understand him yet. If you got to know him, you'd understand that under that gruff outside, he's as soft as a marshmallow inside."

"He hides it well."

"He has to. He gave orders that sent people to their deaths. Do you think a marshmallow could do that?"

"I see what you mean. Is he married?"

"Never married, never had many close friends because he knew the day might come, as it did, that he'd have to send those friends into battle and maybe their deaths. His last words to me before we entered battle with the Russian tanks was, 'Neal, be safe out there.' Either he knew Putin was going to use the bomb, or he had a feeling. Those who spend a lot of time in combat develop a sixth sense. We get a feeling up our neck that something is wrong. That feeling saved my tanks a few times. He has one too. He won't tell me what he feels, so I know it's bad."

"What do you think he knows?"

"I have no idea. He's looking at us, he wants to restart the presentation."

Davis approached me, "Sir, I'm sorry I took a longer break."

"No problem. This is a very sad issue we're discussing."

We returned to review the timeline of the war. I noticed Neal and Lt. Davis seemed to have become much friendlier during the break. I was glad for Neal. He deserved some happiness, however brief, given his condition.

Chapter 12

Davis continued, "General, I'm sure you remember the confusion and panic that followed the explosion of the nuclear land mines."

"I do. I never considered they were the product of Ukraine. I should have since they had Europe's largest reactors, but it went right over my head. I thought had they been enriching uranium, someone would have noticed. It's not a simple process, and specialized equipment was required. I wonder why no one ever figured out heavy equipment was being shipped to Ukraine. Then again, with all of the military supplies flowing in country, no one would notice a few more crates.

"While anyone can Google how to make a simple nuclear weapon, the formulas for how much enriched uranium was required or how far apart the two chunks of uranium needed to be were never published, or so I thought. Then there's the question of how quickly the two have to be accelerated to form the chain reaction when they meet in the tube. There's also the question of the size of the pipe so the high explosives that sent the two pieces of uranium towards each other didn't break the pipe that would send the uranium out of the pipe. Someone not only helped them, they most likely used the uranium and built the bombs for them. Did we ever find out who helped them?"

Davis slowly shook her head, "Sir, our best guess is Israel. They've denied having any hand in building the weapons or assisting the Ukrainians. We were going to send a team to Jerusalem, but before they left, the Middle East cold war turned hot."

I shook my head at her understatement. "Lieutenant, that's an understatement. I've heard rumors of what happened, do you have details?"

"Sir, around 1900 hours local, Iran launched approximately one hundred missiles at Israel. Israel's early warning systems alerted the country. Civilians were ordered to take cover. The IDF was placed on their equivalent of our DEFCON 1.

"Israel's F-16s and F-35s were armed with nuclear bombs and ordered to fly toward Iran but not to enter their airspace until at least one Iranian missile was confirmed to be carrying a nuclear warhead.

"Israel launched their long-range interceptors, first the Arrow 3s were launched, these were developed by Boeing and Israel Aerospace Industries. The missile is a hit-to-kill system designed to hit incoming missiles outside of the atmosphere. The Arrows struck the initial Iranian missiles and confirmed they carried nuclear warheads.

"The order was given to the fighters, escorted by F-15s to strike Iran. At the same time, Israel's land-based Jericho missiles were launched. There were more incoming missiles than the Arrow 3 missiles could handle, and as the Iranian missiles came closer Arrow 2 interceptors were launched. These were designed to catch any leakers that got past the Arrow 3s.

"Israel was the only country with a multi-layered missile defense network. Leakers that managed to survive the Arrow interceptors were met by the next layer, the David's Sling which was designed to catch missiles in the atmosphere."

"I thought their Iron Dome was supposed to take care of in-atmosphere missiles."

"The David's Sling was designed to intercept missiles as they entered the atmosphere. The Iron Dome and the Iron Beam then engaged any leakers."

I was confused, "What's an Iron Beam? Don't tell me they managed to use lasers to intercept missiles."

"General, that's exactly what they did."

"We could have saved millions had we bought or even produced the systems we helped fund. Can you imagine the different outcome of the war if we had been able to intercept most of the Russian missiles? Our politicians were a bunch of fools. They forgot their first priority was to protect the people who voted for them. What was their real priority? Getting rich, and what did their money do for them? Almost all of them are dead, and none of them could take their money with them. Okay, so Israel managed to intercept most of the incoming missiles, what happened with Jerusalem?"

"One missile, a Russian bird sold to Iran that carried MIRVed warheads and penaids, managed to get through all of the interceptors. The thought was that the Russian missile flew in a pack of Iranian missiles so it could survive to destroy the capital. It carried three warheads, all in the 300 to the 350 kiloton range. The city was destroyed. Those in shelters died either from the shelters collapsing on them or lack of air when massive firestorms sucked the oxygen out of the city. Then there were the deaths from radiation exposure. The estimate is out of the one million that lived in the city, 900,000 died within the first 48 hours."

"How many missiles did they intercept?"

"Their intercept rate was in the 90s. They lost four air bases that had already been emptied of planes. The planes were already on their way to Iran. They lost two naval bases, and a couple landed on the West Bank, killing millions of Palestinians. The only major city in Israel that was destroyed was their capital."

"Tell me about the damage to Iran, and is it true the Israelites salted their weapons?"

"Their Jericho land-based missiles relied on their built-up speed to drive ground penetrator weapons deep enough to destroy Iran's buried enrichment sites. A few were targeted on leaders' shelters. The planes arrived shortly after the Jericho missiles had dug out their nuclear program and the Ayatollah's shelters. The bombs released by the fighters were all set for air bursts to extend the diameter of damage and to blow the deadly fallout from the ground penetration explosions back down. A handful of the bombs were huge, much larger than anything we thought the Israelis had. They were in the 10-megaton range. These were the salted weapons. We never learned what they were salted with. Our overhead birds reported no life, zero. No humans, no animals, no life. Whatever they salted them with was very deadly. We received an official notice that had been sent to over one hundred countries warning us not to set foot in Iran for at least fifty years."

I nodded, "I don't think any of the neighboring countries shed a tear over the destruction of Iran. I'll say one thing, the Bible was correct. Something about the Lord saying if anyone messed with Israel, he'd mess with them. He certainly did that. Iran was turned into a sandbox that no one will be able to set foot in for decades, and by that time, Iran will be a forgotten footnote in history. I wonder how the Palestinians feel after getting hit by two of Iran's weapons. They had many chances to sign a treaty with Israel, now they know if they cross the line, they may disappear as Iran did. Same with Assad in Syria. I bet he won't dare strike at Israel again. I wonder if Israel's quiver is empty."

"Before the missile exchange, we received a note telling us we shouldn't worry about Israel, they had over one hundred weapons left and were working around the clock to build more. They were also reloading their silos with replacement missiles."

"How did they manage to reload their silos? Didn't the heat from the engines burn them?"

"They used a cold launch system like the Russians. They helped design the one we planned to use with our Peacekeepers."

"Okay, so the Middle East is settled for at least fifty or more years. What the hell happened after the various committees reached their decision on where the uranium came from?"

Davis nodded, "We have reports of what happened inside Moscow, and the CIA got their hands on a recording."

"How did they pull that off?"

"Right after the initial exchange a key advisor to Putin realized what had happened, he made his way to Finland and then to Switzerland. He walked into our embassy to ask for political asylum. What was his name?"

"Ivanov. Special Advisor to Putin."

"Let's hear the transcript of what he said and the tape of his conversations with Putin."

"Here we go." Davis pulled an audio file and turned on the laptop's speakers.

"Putin refused to accept that the uranium came from one of his reactors. At first, he blamed various upper people in current and past administrations for stealing the uranium and selling it to Ukraine. He killed over fifty of them. One minister stood up to him and told him the uranium did come from a Russian reactor. Putin ordered him shot when he yelled, 'One we left behind in Ukraine.'

"Putin held his right hand up. 'Tell me more.'

"Sir, we built the world's largest reactor in Ukraine. So, in a manner of speaking, it was our reactor. They must have had outside assistance because even with the enriched uranium, it still takes a lot of work to build a bomb."

"Putin looked at the young minister, 'What's your best guess who helped them to kill thousands of our people?'

"Sir, it had to be one of the nuclear powers, either America, the UK, France or possibly Israel."

"Why didn't you mention China?"

"Sir, China has been an ally. They know if we proved they helped the Ukrainians build the weapons that hurt us, we'd strike them with a vengeance that would destroy them. My best guess is the Americans."

"Very good. I agree with you. If you were one of my advisors, what would you suggest we do?"

"Sir, I'd agree to their cease-fire discussions. As a sign of good faith, I'd pull our troops back into the cities we already control. I'd use camouflage tarps to hide the fact that we're changing troops from the untrained conscripts to Guards divisions equipped with our best tanks.

"I would ask that NATO pull their tanks back to the banks of the Dnieper River. We'll agree not to cross the river if they agree not to cross it. We'll say we can discuss peace in Ukraine when we meet in a neutral country. Of course, we'll send a low-standing member of the Foreign and Defense Ministries, just in case we lose them.

"Now that we have NATO camped where we can see them and they're good little boys and girls, we pay them back. We turn Ukraine into a radioactive, glowing death field."

Putin looked at his young advisor, "Are you suggesting we salt our weapons like the Jews did?"

"Sir, of course not. We share a long border with Ukraine, we wouldn't want any of the fallout falling on us. I'm suggesting we use the new fourth-generation weapons set for airburst to minimize the amount of fallout. We strike Ukraine with overlapping strikes, so nothing stands, nothing lives. We teach the world not to use nuclear weapons against Mother Russia."

Putin nodded, "You know that as soon as our first weapon explodes over Ukraine, the Americans will respond in an attempt to save their little children."

"Sir, who are the American's children?"

Putin laughed, "The Ukrainians. The Americans are their rich parents who give money and tell them to go away and not bother them. The Ukrainians demand more money like the spoiled children they are, so the rich parents send them more money. How would you deal with the Americans?"

"Sir, I'd cut the head off the chicken. I'd strike in the middle of the night on a night we know their president is at the White House, and we strike the Pentagon and the Cheyenne Mountain control center. The strikes will need to be very tightly managed so they land within seconds of each other."

"Not a bad plan except for the strike on their Cheyenne. It's a damn mountain!"

"Sir, we send four Satan IIs, each armed with our largest warhead, the 25 megaton monster. The first strike digs a hole. Not deep enough, but it's a start. The second, with some careful aiming, hits the hole the first one dug. This one digs the hole deeper, but not all the way through the mountain. The third digs the hole into the hollowed-out area, the fourth enters the hole and explodes inside the command center."

"Are you sure we can hit the same hole four times?"

"No, so I'd launch eight missiles as a backup plan. Their interceptors may shoot down a few of them, but they have a limited number of them. If all make it through, it doubles our chances of destroying the mountain."

"Won't they have time to send the launch code before the fourth missile arrives? You can't have one directly follow on the heels of an explosion. The shock wave will knock the following missile off its course."

"Sir, along with the Satans we drop a series of smaller warheads around the mountain to destroy the wires and cables they have running from the mountain. To stop radio communications, we explode EMP weapons over the country. Many won't know until they realize radio comms didn't transmit, and they're in the dark."

"And if Europe responds? England and France have nuclear weapons."

"They've always been a pain in the ass. I suggest we destroy them. We can hit them with a time-on-target so what little warning they have won't be sufficient for them to do anything. If we use submarine launched missiles, their warning time will be less than five minutes.

"Their survivors will be hungry and willing to do anything to feed their children and fill their bellies. We should be able to roll across Europe as soon as the small amount of radioactivity reaches a level that's safe. We'll send trucks marked with their red-cross to show we've come to help them. When asked who hit them, we'll blame the Americans. We'll say the American missiles missed their targets and landed in Europe. None of their experts will survive to dispute our story. We'll say they shouldn't have snuck their noses into Ukraine, to begin with. They entered the mess that led to the use of nuclear weapons because Ukraine was their political money laundry. They turned dirty money into clean money. They couldn't use their bank, so they decided to get involved in a war they caused because all we asked was that Ukraine not enter NATO. The Americans pushed Ukraine towards NATO. We can't have them circle us. How would America react if the WARSAW Pact was camped at their northern and southern borders?"

Putin smiled, "I appreciate the thought you put into this plan. I am appointing you a special advisor to me for the war. You will carry my orders to the Defense Minister who can't plan how to take a shit. You will also carry my orders to the Foreign Minister who only wants to talk. That ministry is full of spies, so only tell them the part about us agreeing to a cease-fire and possible peace talks if everyone agrees to stay on their side of the river. Be careful, the minister may want to kiss you for bringing the plan he's been begging me to agree to for months. Remember to tell them only the parts of the plan they need to know right now. When you tell me everyone is in their places, then I'll issue the launch codes."

"Please issue them from the shelter."

"Don't worry. I will be there, and you'll be at my side. Now go and give my instructions to those fools. From today, you are Special Advisor Ivanov."

"Sir, thank you. It is a great honor to be of service to the Motherland."

I looked at Davis after the recording finished, "Holy shit! Where is this Special Advisor to Putin now?"

"I don't know. I know the CIA has him someplace but so far, they haven't shared the location. They did agree if you wanted to, they'd take you to meet him."

"Damn right, I want to meet him. I want to look into the eyes of the motherf-er who killed billions of people."

"I'll send the message that you'd like to meet Ivanov."

I shook my head, thinking we should have dug a pit and dumped his as into it and forgotten about him.

Chapter 13

I asked Lt. Davis, "There's one point I don't understand. I know it's true but how did the most 'Woke' Chairman of the Staffs ever agree to go around the president's back and quickly issue the orders to put the military on a war footing?"

"There a few rumors, but with the Pentagon gone I'm sure we'll ever know the truth."

"I'll settle for a good rumor, there's a grain of truth in a reasonable rumor."

"Okay, but please remember this is only a rumor. The story goes like this, the other chiefs were getting sick of the Chairman's wokeness and playing games with the PRC so someone arranged a tragic accident with a tractor trailer. The truck struck the rear door where the Chairman sat, the kinetic force of the crash crushed the limo and killed the Chairman. The Chief of Naval Operations took over without telling the president. You can say it was illegal, which is might have been, but the CNO and other chiefs of their services enabled us to defeat Russia."

"That took some real balls, if they'd been caught the people behind the president would have demanded their hides."

"They knew the risk they were taking, and they also knew if the war turned hot and went nuclear, which by all of the intel reports it was going to, none of them or the president who refused to go to one of the shelters would survive. The president demanded there wouldn't be a war and he was staying in the White House or his beach house in Delaware. Either way he would have been killed, either by the nuclear strike on the White House or the tidal wave that swept up the coast."

I nodded and smiled. "I wish I could have been in those meetings when they decided the chairman had to go. I would have applauded till my hands were raw. He was a traitor."

"I can't comment on that point, I have no firsthand information on him. I never met him and I won't comment on if he was a traitor or not."

I asked Lt. Davis, "I understand, you don't have to take my word, but I can tell you, he was very bad news for the country. Do we know how they took out the White House, Pentagon, and our government shelters? I thought we had SAMs to protect the key buildings and shelters."

"Ivanov told us the entire plan he wrote that Putin approved. The plan he wrote was based on a version of their cold-war first strike war plan. He said it was a TOT strike."

I was confused, I hadn't heard the term "TOT" before. "Lt. what does TOT mean?"

"Sorry, it's used when discussing strategic strikes, it means Time On Target. Missiles are launched at different times to arrive at their targets at the same time. A sub launched missile that has a flight time of six minutes will be launched later than ICBMs that have a flight time of 30 minutes so both explode at their targets at the same time.

"Ivanov told us he had to modify the original TOT plan because he knew our missile detection system and long-range radars would detect the launch of most of their missiles, so he suggested to Putin the first strike be carried out by submarine launched missiles to decapitate our leaders. He suggested they order the submarine to move as close to our coastline as possible so the flight time to Washington would be only a couple of minutes, not enough time for us to react. He knew that once our leaders were gone, there would be confusion over who could order a launch. He told Putin their follow up strikes should be in the air as soon as the White House, Pentagon and the Mountain were destroyed and they should target our Minutemen silos, bomber bases and sub bases, lowering our ability to carry out a massive counterstrike.

"The flight time from the sub located off our east coast was only four minutes. The missiles launched, ejected their nose cones, the warheads separated from their bus and they and their penaids reentered the atmosphere at over 15,000 mph. Minutes before the sub launched their missiles Russia informed us it was launching two new satellites. Ivanov was brilliant, he ordered the ICBMs to be launched from their space city. He had the new Satan II ICBMs moved to and launched from the launch pads used for space missions. NORAD saw the launch and marked it up as a space launch. They didn't pay much attention to the two missiles until additional missiles began rising from their launchers.

"It wasn't until the missiles ejected their nose cones and the warheads began tracking to their targets and our launch detection birds screamed of a sub launch that the commander of NORAD realized he'd been tricked. He attempted to contact the White House and the Pentagon, not knowing both had been vaporized. While his staff was trying to contact someone in the civilian government to give him launch approval, the Satan II's warheads began striking the mountain. General Scott said screw this and he issued the launch code just as the other warheads began exploding around the Mountain. Those did their job of destroying the fiber cables that carried the orders from the Mountain, but our launch code was out and our first missiles were rising from their silos.

"The first 25 megaton strike on the Mountain shook the buildings on their spring foundations. The buildings swayed, but everything and everyone was fine. General Scott thought if that was all they could do, they were fine. Then the second, third and fourth warhead struck the mountain. While the follow-on strikes weren't perfect, they were good enough. One issue we and the Russians knew was no live missile had ever been fired over the pole. We didn't know the impact if any the magnetic force would have on the warheads as they began their reentry.

"Both of us had calculated the effect, and it appeared both sides managed to compensate for the magnetic pull. The Russians also used sub launched missiles to strike London to kill the King and Prime Minister. They also hit Paris to kill the President. Both strikes were successful. Once both leaders were killed, missiles covered both England and France in nuclear explosions. The two might crawl back to the 15th century in a hundred years. Putin's hate for Germany resulted in over kill. Over two hundreds turned Germany into a cinder.

"Their short-range missiles turned Ukraine into a steaming, radioactive cesspool. Putin said if he couldn't have Ukraine, then no one was going to have her."

Neal and I were shocked. I shook my head, "Putin sounded like a jaded suitor who wanted to kill his girlfriend who broke up with him. If he couldn't have her, then no one could."

"That's exactly correct."

Davis nodded, "He was a psychopath."

"He was. I hope he enjoys eternity in Hell with the other psychopaths who killed millions."

I took a break. This was a lot to digest in a short amount of time. Neal asked me if I was okay. He said I looked pale. I told him I felt like we were fighting the war all over again.

Lt. Davis continued with her review. "With the president gone and the Pentagon vaporized, and Cheyenne destroyed, Ivanov thought they were safe from a counterattack so he could move to the second phase of the attack. Sub launched missiles took out Mount Weather. They hit it with a ground burst followed by two air bursts. They were wasted weapons as the Congress had been alerted to a potential attack but by the time they got dressed and organized it was too late for them to reach one of the shelters waiting for them. Some were caught in Washington, three sub-launched missiles, each with three warheads took care of the city. Others drove as quickly as they could to Mount Weather only to be caught on Interstate 95. Ivanov had studied the maps and knew which interstate they would have to use to reach Mount Weather so he had ordered the sub to blanket I 95 in Virginia with warheads, all air bursts."

"Jesus, this guy thought of everything. What about Raven Rock and the Greenbrier?"

"They used the same formula, ground or ground penetrating warheads followed by air bursts. They blew the shelters even though no one had managed to reach the shelters yet. A week before the attacks NORAD had begged for an increased alert status, the president had refused. He didn't believe the Russians would do anything outside of Ukraine because if they did, we would have plenty of time to send our leaders to the shelters and we could launch as soon as we knew for certain they had launched at us. The president had issued orders saying that unless we were one hundred percent sure we were under attack we should ride out their first strike and then counterstrike. He thought history would show us being the good guys simply responding to their evil."

"Was he crazy? A first strike could have been a few thousand warheads, what in the world was his thinking?"

"He was going to bring peace to the Ukraine and thus the world."

"I know it's disrespectful, but he was crazy. There's no way we could have ridden out a full strike. Did General Scott's launch order reach our launch capsules in time? What happened in Europe? Why didn't they strike Rome and the other capitals?"

"The only countries with nuclear weapons were England and France so those were the ones initially struck. Both countries had warning radars, they managed to send the alert and launch orders as London and Paris were destroyed. As I said, Germany was completely destroyed along with the UK and France.

"France had one sub at sea, they managed to get another out with a small crew, both boats were armed with 16 M-51 missiles. Each missile was armed with five warheads. France managed to launch a total of 160 warheads at Russia. Ten were targeted at Moscow. The balance was targeted at Russian military bases.

"The UK had two of their Vanguard class boats at sea, each carried sixteen Trident II missiles. Each missile was armed with eight warheads. They struck Russia with 256 warheads. Again, ten were targeted at Moscow. There wasn't any communication or cooperation on a targeting plan between the NATO countries. France hit Moscow, the UK hit Moscow and we hit Moscow. By the end, we were only making the debris dance."

Putin survived long enough to order a massive bombardment of Europe with Russia's short and medium range missiles. Much to our surprise, many of the medium range missiles were MIRVED. Over eight hundred warheads struck Europe. Some countries sheltered under their banner of neutrality, only fallout doesn't follow national borders. A few missiles missed their targets and struck Switzerland, Sweden and Finland. Supposedly all were by mistake.

"We were lucky that General Scott got the launch order out. It was confirmed by two minutemen launch capsules, so the missiles began leaving their silos before the Russian missiles targeted at them reached the now empty silos. All but one of our missile boats were at sea. Remember, the aircraft carriers had been armed with nukes so nuclear bomb strikes were carried out by the Navy's F-18s and F-35s. Most of the Air Force's bombers and refueling planes were already in the air. The Russian warheads exploded over empty airbases. The Trident boat in dry dock managed to launch four missiles before the base was destroyed. The captain, XO and weapons officer had stayed behind to launch the missiles. The captain had told the crew to get as far away from the base as they could.

"The real surprise was the Russian Poseidon torpedo was real. It has nuclear power thus its range was almost unlimited. They launched the monster at our east coast. Ivanov told us he thought if the Poseidon worked as designed then a single weapon could destroy our entire east coast and he could use his surviving weapons to take out our silos, bases and key infrastructure. He didn't know our silos and bases were already empty and our counterattack was already in progress. There had been studies on a large underwater explosion, but no one had exploded one in seventy years.

"The Poseidon was thought to carry a 2-megaton warhead, but the surprise was on us, it carried a 10-megaton warhead. Exploded in deep water it created a massive tidal wave that swept inland, destroying all of our coastal cities from Charlotte, South Carolina to Boston. We'd never seen total destruction on that scale. No one in the path of the wave survived. The wave pushed itself up our rivers and streams. Washington had been destroyed from the missile attack, and then the wave washed over the destroyed city and covered anything that may have survived. It left the debris of the city under thirty feet of radioactive water."

I was shocked, "What a minute, didn't the Russians have the submarine that launched against the White House and the Pentagon still close to our coast when the Poseidon exploded? Surely the missile boat would have been hiding from our anti-submarine boats and planes. How did it survive?"

"To the best of our knowledge, it didn't. The submarine that launched the decapitated strike was a new Birei class SSBM."

"Lt., I'm a tanker by profession what does SSBM mean?"

"Sorry, it's the abbreviation for Submarine Service Ballistic Missile. They're the submarines that carry land attack nuclear-armed missiles. In this case, the order was given to the newest boat in Russia's navy. A Birei class commandeered by Captain First Rank Mikhail Orlov. Orlov commanded the first of class in every one of Russia's SSBM boats in the last ten years. The Birei class carried 16 RSM-56 Bulava missiles. Each missile carried 6-10 warheads with a yield of 100-150 kilotons. Our intelligence said the missiles have an accuracy of between 150 and 300 meters depending on the distance between launch and target. In this case, Orlov was ordered to get as close to our coast as possible. He managed to avoid our attack boats, and since the president had cut the Navy's budget, one item that was cut was our underwater microphones that listened to approaching Russian subs. Orlov managed to get within of fifty miles of our coast when he launched. He and his boat became a sacrificial lamb.

"His boat got caught in Poseidon's explosion. I think Ivanov planned it that way so Orlov couldn't brag about firing the missiles that killed the American President."

Neal nodded, "Cold hearted bastards, weren't they?"

I nodded my agreement, "They were, may they all rot in Hell. Is there any good news?"

"Our 64 ground-based interceptors managed to take down 56 Russian ICBMs and the Navy's SM 3's managed to hit another forty."

Neal asked, "So the general in command of NORAD issued the launch order before he died? Is that how we responded?"

"That's correct. His quick action saved our Minutemen ICBMs. Of the 450 we had in their silos, fifteen were being worked on, of those they managed to get five into the air and the other 440 launched before the incoming Russian warheads took out their silos. The bad news is the Russians hit each silo with two warheads, each was a ground burst. They created tons of fallout that the winds carried east across the Midwest and into New England. With Washington destroyed FEMA never managed to get the warning out. Millions died because they didn't take shelter in time or they didn't stay in their shelter for long enough."

I was really pissed. "So, we hit Russia with what?"

"Each of the Minutemen carried three warheads, that's 1320 nukes, they also carried a new jammer and penaids that completely confused the Russian's S-400 and 500 SAM systems. A few carried high-altitude exploding EMP warheads. These overpowered the Russian networks and knocked out their early warning radars. Two knew how to play this game. A Trident boat, that's our SSBM, General, dropped some warheads into the White Sea where some of the Russian SSBMs were hiding. The good news is we believe we sunk two-thirds of them, but half had already launched their missiles. Three-quarters of our attack boats were on patrol when they received their orders. They went hunting for the Russian boats. According to a report, a Trident boat discovered a Russian SSBM sharing the same patch of ocean. She launched two Mark 48 torpedoes and destroyed the Russian boat.

"I think that's the first time in history a missile boat sunk another missile boat. They're usually ordered to stay hidden. The attack boat that was guarding our SSBM was attacking the Russian's attack boat guarding their SSBM. Our Trident boat was sitting on the seabed, sitting there minding her own business, silent like a hole in the ocean, when her passive sonars picked up the Russian boat. The Russian passed right in front of our boat, whose captain had real brass ones. He put two fish into the Russian boat that then split it in two.

"Our boat then rose to one hundred feet and launched their twenty-four Tridents, each carrying eight warheads, into Russia. 192 warheads, which amounted to a total of 72,000 kilotons of nuclear fury. Our missile boats launched 2,496 warheads at Russia. This is in addition to the 1,320 warheads our Minutemen landed on Russia.

"Then the Air Force took over. The bombers took longer to reach their targets, and they found most of their primary targets destroyed so they went after the secondary, and in some cases they flew around looking for what they considered be to juicy targets. Fifty B-52s carried twelve cruise missiles and eight gravity bombs, which was an additional 1,000 nukes, then the B-1s dropped their load while fifteen B-2s and three B-21s roamed the country looking for targets. All in, I'd say we dropped over 5,000 nukes on Russia. We knew where their shelters were so we gave theirs the same treatment they gave us. Penetrating bombs followed by either a ground or air burst. The bombers fired missiles at any Russian ship they saw. City busting nukes were used on destroyers."

I slowly shook my head, I looked at Neal and then Lt. Davis, "This all sounds great, then I look at this map the captain of the Wasp gave me. Look at the damage shown on this map of our country. Can you explain what the hell happened? Our interceptors nailed 40 plus of their missiles, our attack boats sunk some of their missile boats, and one of our missile boats sunk one of theirs. All good news, then I look at this map, and I say to myself. BS. Tell us the truth. No more sugarcoating with sprinkles."

"Yes, sir. The truth is we got our asses kicked. We kicked the Russian's ass. They kicked Europe's. In a few hours, the northern hemisphere lost over 80% of their population, with more dying every day."

"Thank you for telling us the truth." I thought to myself, 80% and more dying. Her words sent a chill down my back and made me shake. How do you rebuild from that? I remembered the rebuilding of Germany and Japan after World War 2, but this time we have to deal with no central governments, lingering radiation, and millions severely wounded. I looked at the map of the Russian strike on us and the fallout tails. I need a plan when I meet with the president.

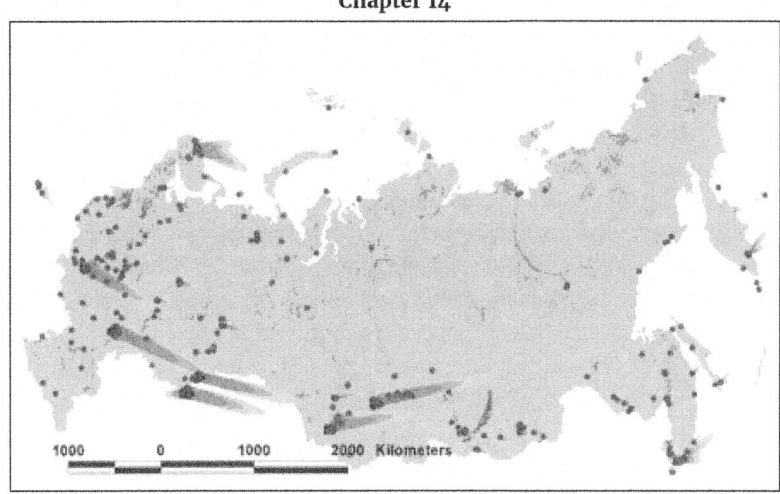

Chapter 14

Just before we landed, Lt. Davis received a map that showed our initial strikes on Russia. She told me, "The cloud cover is too thick for our overhead birds to get a good picture of all of our strikes. Our pilots reported difficulty seeing their targets."

"What did they do if they couldn't see their targets?"

"They said their only option was to drop where their GPS receivers said their targets should be. According to their reports, Russia is a dead country. We dropped a large number of ground-burst weapons to dig out their silos, shelters, and storage sites. We destroyed every naval base they had. We destroyed every Air Force and commercial airport large enough to accommodate a military plane. We paid special attention to their transcontinental railroad. The tracks are melted and twisted, they're totally unusable.

"The UK, France, and of course we hit Moscow, the difference was we hit the city with ground penetrators to get their shelters under the city. We did the same with St. Petersburg, Novosibirsk, Yekaterinburg, Kazan, Nizhy Novgotod, Chegtsd/lyabinsk, Krasnoyarsk, Samara, UFA, Rosov-ns-Donu, Omsk, Krasnodar,Voronezh, Perm and of course Olo. The CIA said most, if not all, most had shelters for high party officials in their city. We destroyed every city and the shelters under them. According to the weapons experts, no one is going to be living in or close to those cities for a generation. A couple of our warheads targeted on Moscow had a special weapon. Upon striking the ground, the nuke intentionally fizzed and spread highly radioactive material in a circle hundreds of yards wide. The ground and under that material will be hot for generations."

I shook my head. "So, between Russia and NATO, we destroyed most of the Northern Hemisphere. We killed millions over an article in an agreement that, in the past, when we asked for our allies' assistance during our war on terror, most of NATO sat on the sidelines. When we asked them to live up to the percentage of GNP they spent on defense, they refused. They wanted to rely upon us to protect them. When we needed to fly over their countries when we were going to strike Libya in the 80's, they refused. Look at the mess we're in now because Poland claimed NATO had to honor Article 5. This was after France said Europe should stand on her own feet and not rely on America. When the bear knocked on their front door, they froze and ran to Uncle Sam."

The pilot announced we were on our final approach when Lt. Davis said, "I just received an update for you, there's an underwater battle going on 400 miles from Hawaii."

I nodded my understanding, "Who are we fighting, the Russians or the Chinese?"

"Sir, the boat involved didn't say, only that there were fish fired on both sides."

We felt the wheels strike the runway, and the engines reversed as we slowed. I saw from the window we were pulling into a hangar that had three LAVs parked in front. I wondered who some of the people were and then I saw him. Our new president. The 47th, the line of succession had worked. He, the Speaker of the House, was now the President. I can imagine the nightmares the left was having, if there's any right or left remaining. I hoped that after the war we're all Americans, but I knew better.

The Secret Service checked the plane and asked Neal and I for our side arms, telling us they'd be returned after our meeting with the president. The hangar had a row of offices and conference rooms on the second floor.

We left the plane and found our way to the stairs and to the right conference room. I looked down and wasn't surprised to see two platoons of Marines and now six LAVs and two M1 tanks guarding the hangar.

Neal and I saluted the president who smiled and showed us where to sit. Someone asked us if we wanted coffee and a small snack. We took both. We knew that too much coffee would upset our stomachs, which was the last thing we needed.

The president surprised us when he told us we'd just caught him before he left. His new Secretary of Homeland Security told us no one liked the president being right on the border with Mexico. They feared a strike by the cartels. I asked where they were going, I knew it wasn't Washington, nothing would be rebuilt until the radioactive lake was drained. The president smiled, his answered caught me by surprise. "Kansas City."

"Sir, wasn't KC hit?"

"It caught a near miss so much of the city survived. That which survived then had to tend with the riots and destruction Antifa caused. I declared them a domestic terrorist organization and any of them could be arrested on sight. We're going to be forced to operate under a condition of martial law so we can help the homeless and wounded, clear the cities and restore peace. General, that's where you come in. Under martial law I can use your troops to restore order."

"Sir, if I may, why Kansas City?"

"General, have you ever heard of the Subtropolis?"

"No, sir. I can honestly say that's a new one on me."

The president smiled and asked his CoS to project a map of KC on the wall. "General, under KC is a vast network of manmade limestone caves. They cover an area in excess of 55 million square feet."

My face showed my surprise.

"Yes, you heard me right, 55 million square feet. Many companies used it to store their documents. In the 1970s Ford used it to store unsold cars. The caves are naturally climate-controlled with a temperature between 60 and 70 degrees year-round. They're deep enough they survived the close by nukes. Their deep enough the radiation didn't reach them. I learned there's an underground river under the mines and we can build air filters to make sure dust and any germs don't enter."

"I had no idea. They weren't destroyed?"

"Nope. I had dispatched an ODA of special forces to check the mines out. They reported miles of filing cabinets and stacks of record boxes reaching to the ceiling and a few homeless living in the caves. Two weeks ago, I sent three platoons of SEABEES and two platoons of Army engineers to work together to clear out the space and begin to turn it into a workable space for the capital to sit. They flew in on a C-130 that could land on the freeway. A second C-130 carried their armored Strikers.

"I told them we can't afford the resources or time to rebuild Washington, but we do need a place to house the new Congress and a new White House. Both can be simple structures, but time was key. They agreed the risk of me remaining right on the border was too risky, so they've been working around the clock to construct a temporary capital for the country."

"Sir, do I want to know where the building supplies are coming from?"

"I told them to be creative. I don't want to know, and I suggest you play it the same."

"Yes, sir." I had visions of a swarm of locust tearing the buildings of KC apart and moving them to the caves. I really hoped I was wrong.

"Sir, how long until the relocation to the mines?"

"I spoke with the officer in charge of the construction just before your plane arrived. He estimated six weeks. My team believes will take us that long to pack and move to the mines. What are your thoughts?"

"Mr. President, you can't be in a convoy for weeks. The risk is too high. People will swarm your vehicles for a crust of moldy bread. I've read reports that there are self-declared warlords that are trying to establish feudal kingdoms, is that true?"

President McCarthy slowly nodded his agreement. "General, the country is in a mess. We're losing thousands a day from all types of diseases, we don't have medications, not even any over the counter. A bottle of aspirin is worth a thousand dollars, if our dollars had any value. Truth be told, I don't think anyone's currency has any value.

"I want you to take command of what's left of our military and National Guard. I need a safe route to the mines, and we need to make sure the sea lanes are clear. I've been told there are Russian and Chinese ships attacking ours, and I want that stopped. If China wants to play, then we'll play. Ten of the Trident boats returned to Mayport, where they're being rearmed and loaded with replacement missiles.

"I was told we have at least fifty of the Peacekeeper missiles stored somewhere, find them, and make them ready for use. I need the riots in what's left of the cities that didn't receive direct strikes stopped, and I don't care what means you use. I've declared martial law so use it."

"Sir, how far can I go to restore order?"

President McCarty grinned, "General, restore order. The sooner the better. I'm not going to open warehouses of MREs and canned food, so warlords' gangs take them to sell to the hungry population."

"Yes, sir."

"Oh, there is one other mission I need your help with."

"Sir?"

"The president of Mexico is complaining that too many Americans are illegally entering Mexico. He wants us to stop them."

"Sir, do you want it stopped?"

"Of course I do," replied the president with a wink of his eye. I got the message. I was to put on a show for the president of Mexico and focus on my core missions. The president said he had sent a general message across the country that he had promoted me and had placed me in charge of the military. He also called up the reserves and asked the recently retired to come to service to help put the country back together.

I didn't want to tell the president that my secure voicemail was chocked full with hundreds of messages asking me NOT to put the country back together but to form two countries, one made up of the blue states and one of the red. The demands came from general officers and even scholars who said this was the best and maybe the only chance we'd have of fixing the ills of the country. I knew if I did what they asked, I'd be considered the new General Robert E. Lee.

We were too weak for a regular civil war, but a peaceful divorce was something I'd have to spend some time thinking about. My first task was meeting with my staff who'd been preparing for my arrival with hundreds of pages of PowerPoint presentations. I'm sure their slides would be so full of small diagrams and symbols that in business they'd have made the military's one chart into three or four.

I'll have to make the staff understand we don't have time for fancy presentations, just give me the data, short and sweet. If I asked for more details, give it to me but don't drown me in data. We can generate so much that it becomes useless.

The president told me the base's commander never made it back to the fort, so his home and office was now mine. He told me good luck and he expected two briefings a day. Lucky me. Why did I agree to accept this position, oh, that's right, I wasn't asked. Time for Neal and I to get back to work and see if we can save the old lady from herself.

Chapter 15

Bryan Webber had been in command of the USS Oregon (SSN 793), a flight IV Virginia class nuclear-powered attack submarine, for three months. He had previously been the executive officer on the lead boat of the class, the USS Virginia (SSN 774). He's spent his entire twenty years in the navy on various submarines.

At present, his boat was both the hunter and the hunted. He was playing a deadly game of cat and mouse with a Russian Yasen class nuclear-powered attack submarine. The Yasen was Russia's answer to the Virginia class.

The Oregon was escorting the USS Tennessee (SSBN 734), a nuclear-powered strategic missile submarine armed with twenty-four Trident 2LE missiles, each armed with ten warheads. The Tennessee had fired her missiles very early in the war. Her targets were the Russian's Pacific military bases. She had been based out of Bangor Trident Base before it had been destroyed by submarine-launched missiles. The launching submarine had been sunk as she was launching her sixth missile.

The Oregon had managed to make it to Mayport, Florida, where she'd been reloaded with fresh missiles and been provisioned with enough food to support a 120-day mission. The Oregon had been the Tennessee's escort as soon as she left Mayport. Webber's orders were to protect the Tennessee at all costs.

They had rounded the tip of South America and entered the Pacific Ocean. They moved slowly and silently to prevent any Russian or Chinese boats from locating them. They had been ordered to take up a position in a box that was 800 miles from Pearl Harbor. The Oregon had caught a sniff of a Russian attack boat when they were on their way to the patrol area. The Oregon had fired a Mark 48 Mod 7 heavy torpedo at the Russian boat who had responded with a snap shot down the bearing of the incoming American torpedo. The Oregon had quickly changed course and left two noise makers in her wake as she turned 90 degrees to port to avoid the spot where Webber knew the Russian would be searching for them.

The two torpedoes had missed their targets. The Russian boat did the same thing as the Oregon. It had launched a noise maker and changed depth and course to avoid the American torpedo. Webber told his XO, Commander Blake Wilson, "We fired from too far away. We gave him time to avoid our fish. Next time I want to be close enough to smell their captain's breath."

"Sir, how do you plan to find him again?"

"We're going to hide in the outgrowth of rocks to our port, then we're going to release one of the new small unmanned sensor packages. We're staying here, so when the unmanned device goes active, we won't be visible to our Russian friend. We'll receive active data that we'll use to shoot the Russian."

"Yes, sir. Are you sure the outgrowth will mask our position when the device goes active?"

"It should, it's large enough to allow us to loiter behind it without their sonar seeing us. We need to be ready to fire as soon as the probe sends us the Russian's position."

"Sir, we will be. Tubes one through three are loaded with Mark 48s, tube four is loaded with a decoy."

"Excellent, now we wait and listen. Commander, keep the boat at silent operations. Whoever hears the other first fires first. I'm going to sonar to see what they hear out there. My gut says we're dealing with one of Russia's new boats that's supposed to be as quiet as our Virginia block 2s. That only gives us a slight edge over them. We don't know what other tricks they may have developed."

Webber entered the dim sonar space. Three people, two women and one man, sat before screens wearing headphones, and a chief petty officer who sat behind them. He watched the waterfall displays that showed every sound the boat picked up and analyzed.

The chief petty officer looked up, "Captain's on the deck."

"As you were. Tell me what you've got."

"Sir, we have the tail behind us, the passive sensors along the hull and the bow have given us a picture of the water around us. There are a lot of outgrowths and mounts for the boat to hide in. The probe that has been launched is silently advancing toward where we thought the Russian boat was. It's currently 2000 meters from us."

"When do you plan to go active?"

"Sir, we have this area of the ocean mapped, that area of the rocks is where I had planned on going active."

"Approved."

The Oregon vibrated from the probe's active pulses. The active pulses caught the stern of the Russian boat, itself hiding behind a mount on the ocean's floor. Webber smiled, "Caught the little bitch. Right where I thought she'd be. Right where I would hide if I were in his position. That pulse most likely also told him where we are. Can we nail him?"

"Sir, that's a question for Weps."

Webber walked back to the command center. "Weps, program one of the fish to swim out of the tube and come toward the Russian boat from the other side of the mount he's hiding behind. Will the control wires hold up with all of these rocks?"

"Sir, if we can keep the fish above them yes."

"Launch the fish and keep the control wires connected as long as possible. Cut the wires when the fish goes active."

The Oregon shook as the Mark 48 was launched a moment later, the sonar tech said, "Fish in the water. It's heading in our direction. It's currently 3,000 meters from us."

Webber looked at the display. "They're trying to do the same thing as us. I want us to rise above the layer, and when we do I want a noise maker and two decoys launched. If we're lucky, their fish will go for either the noise maker or one of the decoys. On my mark, launch the noise maker and decoys, then rapid rise to 150 feet."

The officer of the deck repeated the orders. Webber nodded. "MARK. Launch the noise maker and the decoys. Officer of the deck, rise, rise."

Weps called out, "Sir, we're losing the wires to our fish. She has not, repeat not gone active."

"How far is the probe from where we think the red boat is?"

"Less than 1,000 meters."

"Turn her active and cut her loose. Load tube one with Mark 48s. Drop another noise maker."

Sonar replied, "Two additional red fish are hunting us."

"Sonar are they above or below the layer?"

"One is above and one below."

"Launch tubes one and two, one to hunt above and one below the layer."

There were now six torpedoes in the water, all hunting for a submarine. The Oregon shook from an explosion. Webber asked, "Ours or theirs?"

"Theirs, one went for our decoy."

The Oregon shook again. "Whose and where?"

"One of ours, hit one of their decoys."

"How many are still out there?"

Sonar said, "Sir, we've got them. They also went above the layer, 5,000 meters."

"Snap shot tube three and reload tubes one and two."

"Sir, fish behind us, it's gone active."

"Shit, drop two noise makers and emergency blow. Sound collision!"

Sonar said, "Sir, we got her! Explosion and breakup noises."

Webber thought we got her, and she may get us."

The Oregon shook from a close by an explosion. "Damage report."

"Sir, the fish went for the noise maker, but she was only 200 meters from us. We have leaks in the reactor and gear compartments. Have reports coming in of a major leak in the torpedo room."

Webber said to the officer of the deck. "Continue to the surface. Divers prepare to check the hull when we surface. Radio, send a report to Pearl with our position and a summary of the battle."

"Aye, sir."

"Damage to Captain."

"Go Damage, "The leak in the reactor compartment is getting worse."

"How are the batteries?"

"One hundred percent."

"Shut the reactor so we don't have a coolant leak."

"Sir. We're on the surface. No contacts on radar."

"Lookouts to the conning tower. Radio, get me Pearl."

@@@@@

I was handed a transcript of the Oregon's battle and condition. I handed the report to Neal. He looked at me after he read it. "Neal, get them whatever they need. I don't need red boats that close to Pearl. Anyone of them could lob a few cruise missiles into Pearl and ruin our day."

Neal picked up an encrypted tablet and sent a series of orders and requests to Pearl. A few minutes later, he looked at me. "Sir, an ocean tug is on the way to bring the Oregon home and two Los Angeles boats and the Seawolf that had just completed a sonar upgrade are patrolling the waters around Pearl. The Navy are also sending three P-8s to search for any other red boats."

"Pass along a job well done and tell them are authorized to sink any red boats they locate."

"Sir, he asked if they locate Chinese boats?"

"Warn them away, if they don't, tell them we will sink them if they don't stay at least 500 miles from Hawaii."

"Sir, can we do that?"

"I just did. How many missiles do we have ready?"

"Three Trident boats have been reloaded. Two are in the process of being reloaded, all are in Mayport. None of the minutemen silos survived. The Air Force is looking at other ways to launch missiles. Years ago they did some launches by dropping a Minuteman from a C-17 and they worked with the Army to test a launch from a modified tractor trailer truck.

"We have one hundred Minutemen that had been removed from their silos but not cut up. They are being checked and armed. Boeing is working on putting at least fifteen Peacekeepers back together. They expect to have two a week ready, starting in 6 weeks.

"Sir, their teams discovered one hundred Trident ones in a row of weapons bunkers."

"Remind me what's the difference between the one and two."

"Sir, I had to ask the same question, the one was the original version of the Trident, they have reduced range compared to the 2 which is longer and wider allowing more fuel, giving them the ability to carry a larger payload and have a aero-spike that helps lower drag and increases the missile's range. We don't have any submarines able to launch the ones."

I thought for a minute. "See what else they can be fired from. Normally I'd suggest we check with London, but there is no London or much of Europe left. Ask the bright engineers to come up with a plan to launch the ones, after they get the Minutemen and Peacekeepers ready. Overall, this news is better than I expected. I'll tell the president he can slap the Chinese if they give him a hard time on us kicking his boats away from Pearl."

PART TWO
The Journey to Kansas City

Chapter 1

Neal looked at our available ground forces that we could use to escort the president and his staff to Kansas City. I also needed to make sure the two ODA teams the president had sent had backups in case they ran into trouble. I had asked the staff, what little I had, for an inventory of available ground equipment to convoy to KC. We're looking at a road trip of over 1,000 miles over a highway system that's been through a nuclear war. I needed information on the condition of the roads and what potential threats we're going to run into. I knew a convoy was going to be seen as a treasure by many. They'd know we had food, clean water, and weapons. I'm sure we were going to run into all sorts of trouble and saying we had the president with us would lead to increased violence. The people would blame the president for the war even though he wasn't the president at the time.

I needed feet on the ground to check every inch of the route the president would take. I tasked two ODA teams with the mission of scouting the roads to KC. I issued orders to up armor every vehicle going on the trip and to install extra fuel tanks. We couldn't stop at every exit to fill up. I doubt that any station along the freeway still had any fuel or much of anything. The only thing I was sure of was people would assume, rightly, that we had gas, food and water.

I told the two ODA teams to dress in their oldest, dirtiest jeans and jackets they had. Their commander, Captain Rand, told me they were used to working behind the lines and blending in with the locals. They traded their new M-5s for AR-15s, all had M-16 full automatic lowers in case they had to defend against a mass attack like the Chinese did in the Korean War.

Rand laid out a road map on my conference room table. I laughed, "I guess you won't be using Google maps."

"I never liked Google maps, there were better choices. Today, I'm glad I saved this old Rand McNalley road atlas. Let me show you the route I picked. Route 19 to I-10 into Texas, then pick up I-20 to Fort Worth where we'll take I-35 all the way into Kansas, where we'll pick up I- 335 to I-70, and we're there."

"I wish there was a more direct route. I'm sure you're going to run into trouble along the route. Remember, they're Americans who are hungry and looking for help. Make sure you pay attention to your radiation sensors. Don't drive through hot areas."

"I know they're Americans. We can't carry enough supplies to give much away and have enough for us, and for us to hold the mines waiting for the main body to arrive. I do have a suggestion."

"Captain, I'm all ears."

"Sir, this is a long trip at the worst of times. It's over 1,000 miles, and due to detours it will most likely be over 1,200. I suggest you assemble at least four armored teams to follow us. They should set up forts along the route to protect the main convoy and to help protect the locals from any warlords, or the cartels who are still very active along the border."

"Captain, an excellent idea. I'll have the teams ready when you locate a good location for each fort. I'll send the first to find the first spot. Your team should wait there for the armor, and once they're established, you move to the next spot and so on."

"Sir, that's going to slow the entire trip. Doesn't the president want to be established there as soon as possible?"

"He does, but he also wants to arrive there alive. I can convince him that a delay will both ensure the security of the trip and help the locals."

"Good double play. Sir, when do you want us to leave?"

"When can you?"

"Tonight. I'd normally travel in darkness to make it more difficult for us to be tracked. Since it's important to get the lay of the land we'll have to do most of our travels in daylight so we can get a good impression of the local conditions. We'll be traveling in pickups that have been up-armored and have miniguns and grenade launchers installed."

"We called them technicals."

"I call them, bring the hurt because those miniguns make a machinegun look like it's shooting semi."

Both of us laughed.

"Captain, I'm not sure of the atmospheric conditions along the trip and the distance we're going to get from the radios."

"Have anyone who can read smoke signals?"

I laughed, "Don't I wish."

"I too worried about the comms issue. I gave the problem to my comms genius. He told me not to worry because he'd already, in his words, juiced the power of our radios, so I'll just have to trust him. He hasn't ever let me down before."

"I leave it with you. I'll stop by the motor pool when you're getting to leave."

@@@@@

Juan Labbe, the new master cartel boss, had turned the border into a very lucrative business. He charged people who wanted to go into America, and he charged Americans who wanted to enter Mexico. As he told his number two, "I get them going both ways."

His number two said, "It makes up for the loss of the drug business."

"Don't worry, the drug business will return as the Yankees rebuild. My next idea is to set up toll booths along the freeways, making them toll roads. You want to use my roads, you pay for it. I talked to the cartels in Venezuela, I told them I need gas and diesel. We can make a killing selling the fuel to the Yankees who have working vehicles but no fuel."

"Jefe, that is a brilliant idea. What did they say?"

"At first, they thought I was crazy. Then I explained that none of these pumps are pumping. Their huge refineries in Houston were destroyed in the war, so fuel, fresh food, and clean water will sell better than cocaine. These Yankees are hungry and thirsty. We are going to make more money than we ever did."

"Jefe, more money, but is it worth anything?"

Labbe laughed, "Today it's not even good toilet paper, but I heard the Yankees have a new President. They will begin rebuilding, and when they do, we'll be right there as their friends helping them. We need to help them get back on their feet in order for the billions we're sitting on are to be worth anything. I want to help the Yankees so we can make money from them."

@@@@@

An hour after sunset, I met Rand at the motor pool. He had six pickup trucks, each had sheet steel welded to the doors, fenders, and hood. All of his people were dressed in stained jeans and soiled shirts. Each carried a side arm, and the automatic AR- 15s that didn't show the automatic symbol on the bottoms. I saw the rows of fuel cans mounted inside steel boxes in the bed of the trucks. I also noticed the cases of ammo and MREs.

"Expecting a war?"

"You know the old saying, 'if you want peace, prepare for war.' I don't want to be caught almost to the mines and find out we ran out of ammo. Sir, as an Army man you know that when we're being attacked you can never have enough ammo."

"I agree. Do you need anything from me?"

"General, you've given me a free hand which is all I can ask for. I have the comms schedule our people worked out. My only concern is the cartels."

"Do you think they've moved into southern Texas?"

"I believe they're everywhere. The war hurt their business and left their pallets of cash worthless. They have to find a way to help us back on our feet, so the dollar has some value again, on the other hand, this is a perfect time to take control of a large part of our country. They'll show up with an olive branch in one hand, and they'll be holding guns to our heads in the other."

"I assume you've dealt with them before."

Rand smiled, "Oh yes, and I bet there are a few cartel bosses who remember me. I've been a large thorn in their asses for a few years."

"I couldn't have selected a better officer to lead the way. Captain, go with God."

"General, thank you."

I noticed Rand had installed additional mufflers on his trucks because they were almost silent as they left the motor pool. I could tell, looking in Rand's eyes, he was the right officer. He had a perfect record. I knew he would find the best route for our convoy. His success or failure is going to tell us about our future.

I decided there was no time like now to have dinner and then go back to my mounting pile of paper. I wonder where they found all of the paper. I sort of hoped the bombs had burned up all of the paper. No such luck. Without the networks running like they just to, the military returned to paper. Every day I canceled reports I didn't need.

Chapter 2

Captain Rand and his twelve-person team ran into trouble within ten miles of the base. The trouble was a long line of people walking toward the Fort. His scout truck radioed, "Cap, these people are blocking the road, they're pounding on the truck, and some are trying to climb in. We've closed the windows and locked the doors. Our gunner in the back is using a broomstick to knock people off who are trying to climb into the pickup bed where our supplies are stored. What are your orders?"

Rand paused, he wanted to tell his scout to speed up, but that would end up killing most of the civilians who were Americans and looking for food and shelter. "Sarge, how many people are in the group surrounding you?"

"Maybe a hundred. All look tired, and some have burn marks, some show signs of radiation sickness."

"I'll call the Fort. Try not to kill any, we're going to need every able body we can get to rebuild."

"Yes, sir. So, you just want us to sit here?"

"You can drive off the road and try to slowly get around the group. I'm sure we're going to run into more. It's a mistake I made in not seeing this and creating an ROE plan with the General. I'll pass it to him."

"Yes, sir."

I listened to Rand explain the problem. "Captain, this is my fault. I expected this, and in the rush to get you on the road, we missed discussing this. I'll send a medical truck to meet them and bring them some MREs and water. God knows we're sitting on a large mountain of MREs. Only heaven knows why they shipped tens of thousands of cases here. I have no clue, but better to have them than not."

"Sir, should we wait for the help to arrive or try to break through?"

"You have a loudspeaker, use it to tell them to sit tight, and help is coming. I expect they will be there in an hour. Do not allow anyone to steal your weapons or ammo."

"10-4. Rand out."

"Rand to team 1, tell civilians help should arrive in an hour. Sit on the side of the road. Food, water, and a medical team is coming. They will do their best to help."

At first, the civilians didn't believe the message that help was coming. Then they saw a white helicopter with a large red cross on each door. Rand thought the general is on the ball. That large red cross stopped them from going nuts. He saw that they began to drop cases of MREs and water. I bet they don't even take the time to read the instructions on how to heat them, and they eat them cold. Talk about a lousy meal, but in their shoes, I bet it's the best they've had in weeks. I wish them luck.

"Rand to team 1, our friends have moved off the road. Let's see what other trouble we can get into before the sun comes up."

The scout truck traveled without headlights, using the full moon as the light to see. The soldier riding shotgun used her IR laser and night vision to warn the driver of any hazards in the road. They didn't want to hit anyone or anything. The driver was surprised at how clear the road was, and then he saw a roadblock that stopped traffic from entering or leaving I-10. He called it to Captain Rand. "Cap, we've hit our first roadblock at the entrance for I-10."

"Any armed people around it?"

"None that we can see. It's still dark out here. I can get out and take a look."

"Send the private, Caldwell. Tell her to use her night vision and return fire if fired upon."

"Sir, what about the corporal with the minigun?"

"If you're attacked, you're weapons green, I repeat, weapons green if attacked. Sarge, try not to kill our citizens."

The sergeant turned to look at the private riding shotgun, "You heard the boss. Are you ready for this?"

"I wouldn't be a member of this team unless I was."

"Corp will have an eye on you. If you need help and can't use your radio, flash your flashlight."

"On my way." She slid out of the truck that had the interior light removed so the cab didn't light up when the door was opened. The private turned on her night vision and slipped around a corner and looked at the roadblock. She held up a small thermal mono scope to her left eye. She whispered on her radio, "Sarge, three bodies behind the barriers. There's also a truck, but its engine is cold."

"Slowly advance and see if you can figure out if they're armed or what their game is."

"On it."

She silently moved from tree to tree until she got close enough to hear the people behind the roadblock. "We'll hang out here for another hour, then we'll call it a night. Ruth swears she heard a vehicle slowly coming up the road. They may have fuel or food. I'm sorry. I'm so hungry, and so are the boys."

The private got close enough to see they were armed with shotguns. She tossed a flash bang over the roadblock. She then ran around it and held her AR up. "Drop your shotguns and put your hands up."

"Who the hell are you?" Asked the older man, who was getting on his knees.

"I'm the one asking the questions, who are you, and why did you block the road?"

"My name is Lisa, this is my brother Ron and his friend Lonny. My friend told me she heard trucks. We were hoping they were bringing food and water. We thought if we stopped them here, we'd get first dibs on the supplies. I have two young boys who haven't had a thing to eat in two days."

The sergeant pulled the pickup up to the roadblock. He got out, holding his rifle at the ready. "Private, what do we have here?"

"Three hungry people who have a couple of hungry boys back home."

"Their shotguns?"

"Not loaded. I couldn't find any shells."

The sergeant shook his head. "Stand up. Do you have any idea how crazy it is to point an unloaded gun toward someone who IS armed?"

"Sir, we didn't have any shells left over from the last time we had to fight off raiders."

"Wait here."

He handed them two boxes of shells to the amazement of the three and handed them a case of MREs. "This is all we can spare. If you take the road south, it will bring you right to the Fort. They'll give you some food and water. I'm sorry we don't anything else for you. I want you to take your roadblock down so our friends behind us can enter I-10."

Lisa asked, "Do you think it would be okay for me to feed this food to my boys?"

"Do you know how to prepare them?"

"No."

"Cup open the package and pour some hot water in it and let it simmer."

The three got back in one of their pickups. They attached a chain to the roadblock to pull it apart. The Sergeant called Captain Rand. "Sir, the road is clear. No causalities. Hopefully, our next stop will be the border."

"Keep your eyes open and be careful. Use a drone to watch for any issues on the freeway."

"Yes, sir."

The scouts stopped to launch a small drone to look for other roadblocks ahead. Five miles ahead of them, the drone showed them a line of refugees who were walking in the middle of the road. The private said, "We can't get past them. What do you want to do?"

"I've got to call the captain. Can you send the video from the drone to the him?"

"No. We don't have any cell, the drone's working on a small radio that is connected to us through a line-of-sight connection. It has to be in a line-of-sight to the main body."

"Okay. I guess he's going to have to take our word for it and then decide what he wants us to do. I have a bad feeling this is only the beginning of what we're going to run into. If that's the case the president's convoy will never reach KC. Why can't he fly there?"

The scouts stopped to talk to the people who waved them down. Many linked arm to arm to form a roadblock to force the pickup to stop. The scouts learned this group of approximately 300 had broken off from a larger group that had left Phoenix via route 79. They'd heard from a couple of HAM operators who had generators that the west coast was a no go zone. It had been hit by a number of bombs and one of the Russian nuclear torpedoes had exploded off the coast of San Francisco. The explosion not only send a huge wave of radioactive water flooding Oakland and San Francisco, but also affected the coast up to Portland and down to Long Beach. The explosion off-shore had also caused a series of earth quakes that destroyed most of the coastal cities. Whatever the wave missed the earthquake got. The quake went inland all the way to Bakersfield.

They told us they had lived in the southeast side of Phoenix and the bomb struck the Northwest corner. As soon as they saw the mushroom cloud they decided to head east as quickly as they could.

They tried to drive, however the roads were backed up for miles. One minor fender-bender would back up traffic for twenty miles. There were no tow trucks, no police, no EMS, no help of any kind, so rather than sit and wait to die from the fallout, they wrapped themselves in reflective blankets, the type for camping, and left their cars. Hundreds of others did the same thing.

They told us that too many had been under the fallout cloud and had died in their cars or on the side of the roads. No one touched them, their bodies were left to rot. No one wanted to risk touching them. A few desperate people raided the cars for anything of value, with food and water being the items in the highest demand.

Some who had scavenged the dead ended up sick a few days later and the cycle began again. They told us of gun fights over a half a bottle of water. Mercy was in very short supply on the road. Many called it the road of death.

After Rand called me with the information, I told him to sit tight. I was sending a C-130 to drop a few large tents, water and MREs. I was also going to send an RN which was all I could spare at that time.

Rand told the refugees help was on the way and told them to just sit tight. Some decided they wanted the pickups of Rand's small convoy and this being a very bad decision it ended in the deaths of hundreds. A minigun doesn't discriminate over good and bad, if you're in the firing path, you're dead. The shooting into the line of refugees in an attempt to stop some from shooting, backfired.

Hundreds attacked the pickups. Rand was surprised when some in the refugees opened fire on his people with their ARs and shotguns. A few were armed with lever-action rifles loaded in 45-70 government rounds and a few had bolt action hunting rifles chambered in 6.8 and 7mm rounds. These were able to penetrate the body armor Rand's people wore under their shirts. The gun exchange continued until Rand ordered all of his gunners to fire a quick burst into the air and if that didn't stop them, fire on the mob.

The shooting into the air only enraged the mob who swarmed the pickups. When the smoke had cleared the smell of gunpowder, blood and death continued to linger in the air. One of the dying wheezed out, "You mothers, just wait till you get to Pantano."

Rand, who was holding his left arm that had a through and through bullet wound, looked at the dying man who looked to be in his late 40s. "What do you mean until we get to Pantano, it's a ghost town."

The wounded man wheezed and smiled, "You'll join the other ghosts in the town." Then he died. When the C-130 arrived the RN was shocked at the level of death and the number of wounded who were dying. Multiple hits by 308 rounds usually prove to be fatal. Major Weiss who came on the C-130 to help set up an aid station asked Rand what the hell had happened and why he had opened fire on the civilians.

"Sir, they rushed us. Some were armed. I lost six people to their attack and two of my trucks are out of commission. We lost the MREs and water that had been on four of the trucks and we lost three sidearms."

"Rand, you're a combat vet, how the hell did they get the jump on you?"

"I thought they'd see our help as what it was, a gift of mercy. We asked nothing in return. We only wanted to help them. They didn't believe anyone from the government. Rumors spread like a wildfire burning through dry brush, that we were here to kill them and take their daughters."

"Who started that rumor?"

"No idea. I wish I knew who started it so I could shoot them for all the needless death he or she caused today. These people are hungry, thirsty and scared. Any rumor is believed and if it's going to be like this at every town and village we drive through we have a large problem. We've covered less than fifty miles and look at what we've accomplished. Our own mini civil war."

Major Weiss walked through the rows of refugees. Most were too ashamed to look into his eyes. Every fifth or so person he stopped and asked, "Why? Why would you bite the hand that was trying to feed you. We meant you harm. We only wanted to help you and look at the needless suffering that a stupid rumor caused."

No one wanted to speak to Weiss, most simply looked down. They were sitting in rows Indian style with their legs crossed under them. All of their pockets had been turned inside out so no one could smuggle a small gun in and start the bloodshed again.

The troops had disarmed the refugees. Sitting in the dirt in front of every refugee who was armed was their gun. The magazines had been removed from semi-auto guns. If they were bolt action rifles, the bolt was removed. Shotguns had had their magazine tubes removed. Those who were armed had been separated from the others. Those Rand knew for a fact had fired on his people sat with their hands zip tied behind their backs.

Major Weiss returned to Rand, "Well captain, what do you recommend?"

"Sir, you're going to think I'm crazy but, I suggest we return their guns to them. I bet they're going to need them when they get jumped by outlaws or worse. I, with the Major's agreement, will have a little chat about gun safety and using their weapons in a fire fight."

"Captain, you are crazy, but I believe you're right and I agree with your plan. I'll have the crew continue to set up the field kitchen, and you tell those fools they almost cost all of them a hot meal. I agree with you, we're not prepared to fight our own citizens over an MRE. I understand they're starving, but there has to be a better way."

"Sir, I've been looking for a better plan and so far I haven't found one. I don't have the manpower to fight my way to KC. I don't have enough MREs to bribe my way there."

"I think we should reach out and have a chat with the general."

"Major, I know the general, he will want our ideas. He doesn't like problems dumped on his lap without proposed solutions. If we dump this in his lap, we're both going to be on KP or shit barrel duty for the rest of our lives."

"Damn it. I honestly don't have an idea."

Chapter 3

One of the refugees walked towards Captain Rand. Rand studied the middle-aged man who was slowly approaching. Rand decided he was a Native American based on his skin coloring and his long hair that reached his mid back. Rand waved the man to him.

"I'm Captain Rand, is there something you need or want to tell us?"

"The rumor says you are heading across New Mexico."

"May I know your name?"

"I am called Cloud Walker by my people."

"Thank you. I am sure you understand I can't share our route or orders with anyone. There are still a number of people who would like the nation to fail so they can use the people's hunger as a way to build their own personal power."

"I understand. I want you to know, if you plan to cross into New Mexico on Interstate 40 or 10 you will be caught in a spider's web, a very deadly web."

The Indian in front of Rand had his full attention. In Rand's mind, a spider's web would only translate to an ambush. "Can you tell me more about this web? Are you hungry, thirsty?"

"I am fine. Captain, do you know of the Apache?"

"I haven't met one, unless you come from the Apache Nation."

"I am Sioux. My people and the Apache have been at war for over three hundred years. Using your terms, the war turned hot when the mushrooms destroyed so many of the cities that bordered our nations. Many of the Apache moved from northeast Arizona, southern Utah and southwest Colorado because of the deadly dust we were warned about."

Rand felt his stomach tighten, he thought he already knew the answer, but he asked it anyway. "Where did the Apache settle?"

"Along the Arizona and New Mexico border. They have claimed thousands of acres, most of the livable sections of New Mexico as their nation. The rumor is they don't allow any white men to enter their nation."

"How could they stop white men from crossing their nation?"

"They are heavily armed. The rumor says they raided many National Guard armories. They stole the trucks that they filled with the weapons stored in the armories. They even took bulldozers and cranes that they used to build roadblocks. The rumor said they don't allow anyone into their nation unless they are native Americans and then, unless they can prove they are Apache they have to pay a toll."

I said, "I thought the Sioux were a great and mighty nation, why didn't you defeat the Apache?"

"Once we were a mighty nation. Once our war chiefs, Sitting Bull and Crazy Horse defeated your mighty General Custer."

"He was a Colonel at that time."

"His rank means nothing. At the time he was a mighty war chief. He suffered a sickness many war chiefs suffer. They believe they can't be defeated, and their fame will carry them from victory to victory. Such people are easy to defeat. Such people are easy to bait which is what our war chiefs do. That was a long time ago. Our nation was ultimately defeated. White Men like you broke the treaty we signed at Fort Laramie in 1868. Your great and wise judges decided the white man had stolen our lands and we were owed compensation. We refused your money because we wanted our land back.

"After the many mushroom clouds ate the white man's cities, we and the Apache smoke the peace pipe. For the first time in many years, we are peace."

"What did your people offer to the Apache and they to you as an exchange of the smoking the pipe."

"You are a strange white man, you know some of our customs. How did you learn them?"

"Before the mushrooms came, I lived next to one of your reservations outside of Denver. I had many Sioux friends. What can I do for you Cloud Walker?"

"It is not a question of what you can for me. It is a duty I have to bring you a message from the great Apache war chief."

Rand didn't like the sound of this. He was worried the Apache wouldn't allow the president's convoy to transverse New Mexico. "I am listening, what message do you carry from the Apache war chief?"

"If you cross the border and invade the lands of the Apache nation, all of you will be killed. You will be hung on poles that will form a fence across the Apache's border."

Rand thanked Cloud Walker. When Rand was alone with his lieutenant and three sergeants, he told them of the discussion with Cloud Walker. One of the sergeants asked, "Do you really believe this story? I thought there were only a handful of Indians left and those that were left were getting fat from the money the gambling brought them. People who are getting rich don't usually go to war and risk stopping the spigot that's feeding them."

Rand looked at the sergeant, "How many of those casinos do you think survived and who's going to risk traveling through the fallout to go to one? I bet there's not a single casino operating. It's the same with Las Vegas. While the city itself wasn't hit, the fallout from California turned Vegas into a ghost town. I take Cloud Walker's warning very seriously. The Apache and the Sioux were vicious fighters. I think we're going to stay right here until the General decides what he wants to do. I do want some drones flown across the border so we can see firsthand if there is a roadblock at the border and if there is, what's sitting behind it."

One hour Captain Rand learned there was a roadblock at the border and there were warriors in defensive positions behind the roadblock. The drone couldn't report anything else because it was shot down.

Rand thanked his staff and decided not to waste another drone that would most likely be shot down too. He did decide to see if he could contact me. Unfortunately, the atmospherics didn't want to cooperate with him, so he sent a messenger on a Honda motorcycle to bring his report to me.

I read Rand's report and handed it to Neal for his thoughts. I silently wished we had a Secretary of State or Homeland Security so I wouldn't have to deal with his. Neal looked at me, "The Indians are itching for another war between us. Don't they know they can't defeat us and you're no Custer who's going to be caught in their trap? Boss, what are you thinking?"

"I could send a few platoons of tanks into New Mexico, but I really don't want a war. I had to delegate up, but when it comes to nations looking down the barrel of a gun, it's time for the president decide how he wants us to act. Once we get his orders then we'll act. I won't act without his orders. Even if he tells me to use my best judgment, at least I informed him of the risks."

Thirty minutes after the president had received my report and recommendations, he asked to speak to me. His first words, "The Apache want war with us?"

"No, sir. They want us and everyone else they don't approve of to stay away from their nation."

"Don't they realize their nation is in a state of the Union, and they can't just claim a state and declare it as their nation?"

"Sir, the treaty we signed with them at Fort Laramie in 1868 was deemed breached by the Supreme Court."

"General, whose side are you on?"

"Sir, the side of the law."

"The law is a little different after the war. We lost two-thirds of our people and I'd guess, more than 90% of our infrastructure. I can't afford to give away an entire state. I think it's time we have a chat with their war chief and discuss how we can give them what they want and we get what we need. I want you to lead a mission to their roadblock and see if they can get a message to their chief to agree to meet me."

"Yes, sir."

"General, don't do anything stupid. It took me long enough to find a general I thought would do the right thing. I don't want to lose you."

"Thank you, sir."

Chapter 4

As if I didn't have enough on my hands, I was given a report that one of the cruise ships we 'rented' was sunk by a submarine. I guess one dollar counted as rent. Damn it, I thought we had gotten all of the Russian boats. Did the Navy miscount, or did they count underwater explosions as hits? Their torpedoes could have struck underwater outcrops of rocks. I need to have a heart-to-heart with the acting Chief of Naval Ops. I gave him the job because I thought he'd shoot straight with the president and me. I wonder how many other boats had been reported as sunk but weren't. I also worry that we're not dealing with Russian boats but Chinese boats that are pretending to be Russian. Years ago, the Russians sold a number of Kilo boats to the Chinese.

I really hope it was a rogue Russian boat and not a Chinese boat. That would start a war between us and China. We can't afford to go to war with the Chinese after the war with Russia.

I was drafting my response to the CNO when he called to tell me, "General, we got the enemy sub. One of our attack boats, the Seawolf sunk the enemy boat."

"Admiral, whose boat was it?"

"Chinese. It was an SSK."

"I'm not familiar with that term."

"It's a conventionally powered boat. They can be very quiet. The Seawolf heard her opening her torpedo doors."

"You have proof she was a Chinese boat, and she's sunk."

"Our proof is our sonar tape, and our proof is also our tapes that recorded the breaking up sounds of the boat."

"Good. Please send me the tapes so I can use them when the president and I talk to Beijing."

I told the CNO to locate and sink one of China's carriers to make up for the loss of our people on the cruise ship they sunk. "Admiral, make sure China knows why we're sinking their carrier."

"Aye, sir. I'll make sure they know it was us and why."

"Excellent. When you sink it, record it and send me the recording."

"Sir, that means our boat will have to surface to record the sinking."

"Can't the boat's periscope record it?"

"Only if we're close enough. The Mark 48s have a long-range, as do our Tomahawks."

"I don't care how your boat's captain does it, we need a recording of the sinking."

"Aye, sir. I'll find a way."

I'd hoped the Chinese would be sensible. We didn't need another war while we had the issue of the border. According to the detailed report we received, the Indians hold not only the border of New Mexico, but they also control most of New Mexico. I half expected the Native Americans would use the war to rebuild their nations. I didn't think they'd attempt it so quickly. I'm amazed at how quickly they managed to move.

What really caught me by surprise, but it shouldn't have, was the cartel's control of the entire Texan border from El Paso to Brownsville. They're charging Americans entry fees to Mexico, and they're turning many into slaves.

If we ended up in a battle with the Indians, we'd then have to face the cartels, or they may even come to the aid of the Indians. The cartels turned Mexico into a narco country. They own all of the Mexican military's equipment, and intelligence said they've been buying weapons from China to arm them on their march south to conquer Central America.

I also learned the cartel, I should remember to drop the 's,' did something I never thought was possible. They elected a single leader who merged all of the cartels into one. Any cartel leader who refused to follow the new leader was disposed of. They killed him and his entire extended family. They used Mexican Air Force pilots and planes to drop bombs on the ex-cartel leader's home with him and his family in it.

The new leader, Juan Valdez, had worked his up through the cartels. As a young man, he had been marked for a leadership position and had been sent to Harvard and Cambridge to get the best education. He was taught banking, economics, and, most importantly for his future, World History so he could learn from the mistakes that had been made through time.

Valdez had learned the drug business while investing the billions of cash the cartels had on hand. He hired a private military, primarily members of the Mexican military. He paid special attention to hiring Special Forces so he could use them to sneak into the cartel leaders' homes. While NATO fought the brief Third World War, Valdez used the confusion to strike. In one hour, he was the cartel's leader. He used his newly acquired Air Force to make him the sole leader. He used his private army to demand an oath of fidelity from the cartels' soldiers or he had them killed.

His next move was to capture the border between Mexico and Texas. He knew the rich Americans would do anything to escape the fallout and destruction from the war. He killed the surviving American border guards and Texas Rangers. He then quickly built a series of toll booths along the border.

This intelligence worried me. I needed to get Neal to do an inventory of all of our fighting vehicles and the number of trusted soldiers. I thought we could cut a deal with the Indians to allow us to cross their

Nation, and I was sure a deal wasn't going to be easy or even possible to sign with Valdez. I didn't know what his game was, there weren't enough people left in America to use his drugs. On the other hand, we could use some of them to help ease people into a peaceful death. There are millions who are painfully dying from radiation poisoning. It might be an interesting topic to discuss with the president.

I was interrupted by Neal, "Sir?"

"What do you need?"

"We've managed to contact two of the K-14s. We were able to reposition one to look at New Mexico and the Texan border with Mexico."

"That's a bit of good news. How did they get the long-range comms working? I thought the EMPs killed all of them."

"The base had spares stored in a Faraday cage in case of a nuclear attack. We discovered all sorts of radios and test equipment in the sealed room located in a sub-basement."

"That's the best news I've heard since we got here. Have you managed to get any images from the birds?"

The intel specialist looked at me like he'd seen a ghost. "Yes, sir. We've received images. If you'd like, I can show them to you."

"I thought that was why you were here. May I see them?"

"Yes, sir." He looked very nervous.

I took his tablet so I could see the images from the overhead birds. I zoomed them up to see the details. I was amazed at everything I could see. I could even make out the license plates and the marks on the trucks' doors. I didn't like what I saw. The Texas border was being patrolled by Mexicans. They were using Mexican army vehicles, most with heavy machine guns on them. I even saw a handful of Mexican tanks and wheeled vehicles armed with 105mm cannons. Same type we used on our initial M1 tanks. The only thing that makes any sense is that the cartels completely run Mexico and maybe a few other countries.

I also saw a line of Americans, thousands of them, waiting to cross into Mexico. They were funneled through a border control station. Most of the items they were carrying when they reached the border were taken as an entry tax to enter Mexico. Most of the men were loaded on buses and taken who knows where. The young women were loaded on a different group of buses. The very old were taken to the side of the border station and killed. The images clearly showed the rows of the dead being pushed by a bulldozer into a large mass grave. I knew they were taking the men to be their work slaves, and the women were going to end up as pleasure women for their people. Some would most likely be used to breed a new generation of soldiers so Valdez could continue his conquest of the Americas.

I haven't been able to reach anyone in Canada's government yet. They had thought they were safe. They quickly learned they weren't when the Russians struck most of their major cities. Their foolish Prime Minister had told his people they had nothing to worry about as the war was between America, Europe, and Russia. To protect Canada, he had withdrawn Canada from NATO.

I guess the Russians didn't see the message. A number of their missiles deposited death across Canada. Many of the Canadian survivors tried to enter America only to discover more damage and death. The Canadians were passed by rows of Americans attempting to make their way to Canada. When the two parties met on the road, they exchanged information. Both parties realized they had nowhere to go. They decided to look for a new place to settle. They decided to settle by a river or lake that had fresh water. They'd hunt for food until they could locate seeds and till the land. They make a list of the tools they need to make cabins to settle in. Two hundred and seventy-five years ago, settlers looked for the same places, close to fresh water and suitable to grow crops.

I thought to myself that without power, we were going to revert to the settlers who founded our nation. The major difference, the original settlers knew how to live off the land, we didn't. The DHS once projected that a series of EMP explosions that wiped out our power would lead to 90% of our citizens dying within a year. I wonder what percentage they put on a nuclear war combined with the EMP explosions.

While I thought we could reach an agreement with the Indians, I didn't think we could reach one with the Cartel. That meant war. A war we're not in a position to fight. We still had some nukes, but the president was opposed to using them unless someone used them on us first.

I called all of my officers to meet me in the conference room. I wanted to lay out the problems we faced and hear their thoughts on how we could proceed. The young intel tech explained the situation we were facing with the Native Americas sitting on the border of New Mexico and the Cartel controlling the border with Texas and Mexico. Some thought we should let things be as they were because our first goal should be getting the president to a safe location and rebuilding the federal government. A handful said if we didn't deal with the Indians and Mexicans with all our might, both groups would extend their control over more and more territory.

I told them we would not accept having to bargain for our own land. Later that night I met with President McCarthy. We shared steaks from a fresh kill while we discussed our options. I told him we had to reach an agreement with the Indians before we tackled the Cartel. I suggested we task one of the K-14s to keep an on Valdez so we could build a database on his movements. He agreed and signed the orders.

Moving satellites was a big deal, involving using priceless fuel that we couldn't replace. We'd lost the launch pads in California and Florida, and the destruction of the Cape in Florida meant we lost their launch abilities. The attack on Houston cost us NASA's headquarters, and the loss of Cheyenne cost us our central monitoring site. While the president was chewing, I threw out a suggestion that took him by surprise. "Sir, I believe it might be time to nationalize SpaceX and their launch pads and their available rockets. We need to replace our overhead birds and replace our lost GPS birds."

"Tom, it sounds logical, but I don't like the idea of us rebuilding by nationalizing companies. I would like to ask Elon to join us and see if we can reach an agreement."

"Sir, did he survive? I know Twitter and the rest of social media sites are offline because the internet's servers were destroyed. I guess Putin didn't like being called names and having memes made of him."

"He's alive, he's reached out to us. He requested a meeting. I was about to ask you what you thought. Before we discuss it, even if we had his launch vehicles, we don't have anything to put on them."

I smiled like the Cheshire Cat. "Sir, yes we do. The DOD didn't really spend millions on toilets. Much of those funds went to the building and stockpiling of needed birds in case we ever got into a shooting war with Russia or China, and they decided to knock out our birds. The plan was to wait until the last birds had flown before taking inventory of the overhead assets before we replace them. We have three K-14 birds and five of the latest generation GPS birds in storage."

"Do you have any other toys hidden away I don't know about?"

"Sir, you know about the missiles and warheads. I have issued the orders to the Bone Yard that survived to make the stored B-1s, F-15s and F-16s brought back to service. We lucked out in the missile or missiles targeted for Fort Worth that would have hurt us in fighter production missed. Lockheed has informed me they are resuming production of the F-35 in three weeks.

"I sent a special team to Groton and Norfolk to see if any of the tools used to make our submarines were salvageable. These people will have special suits and will limit their time in the hot zones. If we can't save the tools, we won't be able to build another submarine for up to five years. Russia failed in striking Pearl. Our THAADs and Patriots knocked down their incoming so I'm looking at what needs to be done to move most of our ship servicing there."

"Why not Mayport?"

"It's just too a small a base. They don't have any of the large dry docks need to repair our surviving ships and subs. Pearl has dry docks and the trained manpower we need. Mayport also has a problem with manpower. Many lived in the suburbs of the base, neighborhoods that were destroyed by direct attack or deadly fallout."

"Can you protect Pearl if the Chinese decide this is their time to strike?"

"Sir, I wanted to get your permission for a project to show the Chinese we're not out of the game and they better not pick this time to cause trouble."

"I'm all ears."

President McCarthy smiled and nodded his agreement. "Tom, I like it. Ballsy and should show Beijing we mean business." The president finished a beer and looked at me, "Tom, level with me, what do you think the Indians want and is China going to use the war to advance their march to ruling the world?"

"I believe the only way to reach an agreement with the Indians is for a face-to- face meeting between you and their chief. We hold the meeting from a position of strength. We have your back with a few platoons of M1 tanks, LAVs and Strikers. We show them that if they want a fight, it won't be on horseback. We'll crush them. We can fly three B-52s over the meeting to show them we're still a force to be reconnected with.

"As for China. I believe we're going to have to fight them sooner or later. My goal is to delay that fight as long as possible so we're in a much stronger position. They don't have a good grasp on our real situation. The skies have been too smoke-covered to give their birds a clear picture of what's going on. That's to our advantage because if they saw the amount of destruction, they would most likely strike. My plan should make them pull up and decide they don't want to take us on right now."

"Have you heard anything from inside Russia?"

"They're tearing themselves apart. They have no national leaders, no food and every one of their cities are in ashes. Warlords are popping up and taking control over sections of the country. Sooner or later these warlords will fight with each other further weakening them."

"I agree. I enjoyed this. We've both been so busy, let's make this a weekly event so we can catch up with each other. My daily briefs give me a decent overview, but I enjoy going back and forth with you. You don't flavor the truth or add politics to it and that's something I really appreciate. You have my approval to move your plan with China ahead and tell me when we're going to meet the Indian chief so I can put it on my calendar."

Chapter 5

I sent a message to Captain Rand to request a meeting between our president and the Apache chief. He informed me their chief would be honored to host our president and would like to give him a tour of the progress they've accomplished in rebuilding two of their cities. I was shocked by the offer and accepted for the president. I learned the two towns were what we had called Lordsburg and Deming. The main meeting would be held at Deming.

I sent a list of the vehicles and people we would be bringing to the meeting. Rand informed me they requested we don't bring any heavy armor vehicles so as to not scare their peaceful people. I reached out to the head of the Secret Service with the news. I knew he would refuse the request because he wanted a large show of force and in case the Indians tried anything, he was prepared to stop it before it got out of hand. Translation, he could use the machine guns and cannons to kill anyone he viewed as a threat. I knew I was going to have to ask the president to have a heart-to-heart chat with his protection detail. I stepped back and realized I'd made a mistake. If I was in the Apache's shoes I wouldn't trust negotiating with someone who brought a platoon of tanks and Bradleys. I think the eight-wheel vehicle was a much better choice. We can explain to the Apache the need to use an armored vehicle because of the cartels attacking along the border and the many outlaws and warlords.

Three hours later Capitan Rand told me the Apache had accepted the LAVs and they were very familiar with them, as they owned a dozen of them. They also inquired about some spare parts they needed. I thought the only place they could have gotten their hands on them was if they'd raided some National Guard armories. If that was the case then they were much better armed than I originally thought. I passed the word that every member of the president's protection detail would be armed with the new M5 rifles and the new class IVA body armor. I wish we had more than the one hundred sets of the new armor. A 7.62 round didn't faze the new armor, even .338 rounds couldn't penetrate the plates and they were lighter than the old.

The meeting was set for a week from today which gave me time to work on my special project for the Chinese. I gathered the best coders, gamers and graphic designers we had. I explained what I wanted, and they had a week to produce it. I left the meeting to a bunch of groans.

I told Rand we were sending him his team uniforms, new body armor and their M5 rifles. They could change back into uniform, and they were going to be part of the protection detail. I also hinted they should shave and trim their hair or keep any pony tails tucked inside their helmets. Rand laughed and replied he would take care of it. He asked for a pair of very sharp scissors. I complied and smiled thinking of what was about to happen in his camp.

A week later twenty-four LAVs pulled up to the border. Behind a series of low hills was a platoon of M-109s and a platoon of MLRS launchers. The MLRS were loaded with the long-range missiles that had a range of over 250 miles. The M-109s were armed with the rocket assisted Excalibur rounds that would lock onto a laser targeting system 40 miles away. As we moved deeper into New Mexico, the M-109s would follow. There were many off ramps and hills for them to hide behind. They would move at night and their engine's had an enlarged muffler installed to make them very quiet.

Our covey was met by six of the Apache's LAVs. The president, Captain Rand, now in his ABU, (Army Battle Uniform) and I walked towards the border. There were twenty-five-armed people behind us. Captain Rand held up a white flag to show we came in peace.

Three Apache, all wearing large head dresses and also carrying a white flag met us on their side of the border. Captain Rand introduced us, the Apache introduced their people, their chief, Fire Maker, their war chief, Slayer of Evil Spirits, and their administration chief, Dust Eater.

Fire Maker welcomed us to their nation and invited us to cross the border in peace. We offered to cross on foot and our LAVs follow. We also asked if we could bring the truck that was loaded with supplies we thought they might have use of, such as medical supplies, squaw personal health items and the spare parts for their LAVs they had requested. Fire Maker smiled and waved the truck forward. He thanked President McCarthy who thanked Fire Maker for agreeing to the meeting.

When we reached Lordsburg, we stopped and gasped in surprise. What was a small run down town that relied on traffic stopping on the interstate was now a town with new homes, admittedly very small ones, but houses. Shops and even a couple of restaurants. We noticed both Indians and whites walking down the sidewalks and going in and out of the shops.

President McCarthy asked, fearing the answer we all knew in our heads.

Fire Maker smiled, "I will confess to helping ourselves to them from empty stores along our route."

I asked, "What about the potential of fallout?"

"There was some. We had a few Geiger counters, and any that were contaminated we tried washing a few times until the counter said they were safe, then we dried the clothes and boots and presto we had inventory."

"What about the people whose stores you raided? Did you pay for their inventory?"

"I fear most died. We buried hundreds in mass graves. We did not know their names so we placed the symbols of the Cross, Jewish star and the Muslim symbol in front of the graves. We also listed the number of people we buried and where we found them. Maybe someday you or someone else will want to know what happened to the people of the empty towns."

I looked at the projected fallout, "I assume most died from the fallout."

"We agree with that. Some had bullet holes in their heads, our medicine man believes they got so sick they took their own lives. The great spirit will decide their true fate. We could leave their bodies to rot where animals would eat their flesh and get ill. One of your people or mine might have killed such animal not knowing they were sick, thus the person eating the animal's flesh might get ill and die. We did a favor to future generations."

"How did you manage to build so many homes so quickly?"

"We didn't build them. There was a company in Colorado that makes them. We sprayed and washed them until the counter said they were clean then we loaded them on trucks and brought them to our people. They do not mind tiny homes as your people would. Mine are happy to have a real roof, one that doesn't leak over their heads."

I asked, "What are your stores going to do when the stolen inventory runs out?"

"As we emptied six large warehouses from Walmart, Target, and Amazon, we should be fine for a while. I hope we will be able to reach a peaceable treaty, and as you rebuild, so will we, we can then become new customers for the rebuild companies."

Rand asked, "Won't the chains you stole from want payment?"

"I think not. They will have either written those loses off like they will do with the stores destroyed in the struck cities or as I think more probable, they will start with a fresh beginning. If I were in your shoes Mr. President, I would be writing the bills that allowed your companies to start fresh or they will write off their loses for a generation and never pay a penny of your taxes."

President McCarthy smiled, "You are a very smart man. We are discussing that very bill."

Fire Maker smiled, "Maybe I have found a smart white man who may be trustworthy and not full of their own ego. Most of your politicians I met before the war always greeted me with their hands out. They thought we were all rich from our casinos."

"I am not like the others. My goal is to rebuild America and make it a safe place for everyone to raise their children. A country that can learn from the mistakes the world made in the Third World War."

"Very well said. Come, let's visit Deming. We will dine there and afterward with full bellies we will talk about what you and I both want. We'll see if we can peacefully coexist and learn to be good neighbors."

Deming was a larger example of Lordsburg. Here rows of new houses were being built. A couple of factories were being retooled to produce things Fire Maker wouldn't share with us. I had a feeling they were building the tools they need to support an army. An army to fight us if we didn't come to an agreement. The one thing we didn't need was a war inside our borders since most of our troops and Marines were spread around the country trying to put down the rise of the warlords. It seems every few towns had their own warlord.

It was going to take us more time than we wanted to admit to clear the country of these scum who preyed on the needy and hungry. I'd issued orders to the soldiers and Marines they were weapons free and use any amount of force they deemed necessary to remove the warlords. As one Marine I overheard tell his buddy, "We're the Raid, and they're the bugs. We're going to crush their asses." Many warlords were nothing more than gang leaders.

The meeting continued for three days. It went back and forth until both leaders decided it was in the best interest for the entire country that they remain friends, and they reach an agreement that each side could live with.

Fire Maker wanted all of New Mexico and most of Arizona. We wanted to call whatever land they got a reservation and not an independent nation. We wanted them to agree never to own weapons of mass destruction. We couldn't accept a nation that might be our friend today but decide at a future date they wanted more and had WMD. That would be allowing a house guest to have dinner at your house while holding a gun to your head.

The final draft, I said draft because it was more of an outline than a full agreement, in which the staff on both sides would remain behind and insert what I called the BS legal language.

Fire Maker and President McCarthy agreed to
- The Native Americans could manage the state of New Mexico, which would be a Native Nation within the United States of America.
- The Native Nation could be self-ruling under the condition that it did not create laws that contradicted the US Constitution.
- The Native Nation had the right to call their leaders whatever they chose.
- The Native Nation would have two senators and a number of house members to be determined by population.
- The Native Nation could have their own military so long as they agreed to use their military in defense of the US if the United States was ever invaded.
- The Native Nation agreed not to use their military to invade the rest of the United States.
- The Native Nation agreed that if the existing population of the state of New Mexico wanted to remain, the Native Nation would not use force to push said population out of their homes and business. Such force including not raising the taxes on those who stayed behind.
- The government of the United States would offer compensation to the existing population to relocate to another state.
- The United States agreed to come to the aid of the Native Nation if they were ever invaded.
- Neither nation would toll the population of the other if they wanted to travel through the territory of the other.
- Each nation agreed to do their best to capture criminals who crossed the borders to escape capture. Said captured criminals would always be returned to the respective nation.

- The Native Nation to teach English to the young in addition to the teaching of their native language.
- Each nation agreed to offer aid and assistance to the other in times of natural or man-made disasters.
- Each nation agreed to honor the religions observed by the populations of the respective nation.
- The population of the Native Nation, if counted by the US Census, would be allowed to vote in US elections. Citizens of the United States would not be allowed to vote in elections within the Native Nation, unless they resided in the Native Nation for more than one year.
- Both nations agreed to honor the borders of the other.
- If the owners of the existing structures and businesses didn't personally claim them within a period of three months from the signing of this agreement, those structures, land, and businesses would become the permanent property of the Native Nation. The Native Nation had one year to remove all property from the location of their previous reservation.
- Each nation agreed not to make counterfeit money used in the other country.
- Citizens of both nations can bank in either or both nations as long as they obey the laws of each nation.

President McCarthy signed the draft; I signed as a witness and the captain sat in a daze not believing what he'd seen. Before we left to return to our base, the president asked Fire Maker if he could arrange for his convoy through New Mexico. Fire Maker smiled, he patted the president on his back while assuring him no harm would come to him while in the Native Nation.

As we were leaving the conference room, the president dropped the intel of the Cartel that was now on the border between Texas and Mexico. He asked Fire Maker what he thought about that. Fire Maker looked pale; he asked his war chief about it who replied he had heard rumors but had no proof.

The president asked me to show them the photos I had that showed the border and the Cartel's operation.

The Sioux were shocked at the clarity and detail of the photos. Fire Maker asked, "Do you have any information of what their plans are?"

I looked at the president who nodded his head, "Sir, we believe and have radio intercepts that indicate they would like to take over all of the southwest."

Fire Maker's face turned red, "Including our nation?"

"Yes, sir. I'm afraid it does."

Fire Maker nodded, "I now understand why you asked to include the section that both countries would come to the aid of the other if invaded. You already knew there was a threat to my new nation. What do you want from us?"

Again, the president nodded to me, "Sir, we'd like permission to base some of our attack and fighter planes on your airports. We'd like to use your border with Texas as a jumping-off base and to store supplies close to the front."

Fire Maker looked at his people, who nodded their agreement. Fire Maker asked, "I believe we should do more than just give you the right to base your planes and people at our bases or airports. I know you will lease them, thus paying us for the time you're there. You'll also buy fuel from us. You'll be helping us by using our bases. I would like to offer some of our warriors to fight alongside yours."

The president hid a smile while extending his hand across the table to shake Fire Maker's hand. "Sir, if it is okay with you, General Morton here will coordinate our plans with you."

"Excellent, I believe this is a perfect time to bring back an old-time honored act, we will smoke the pipe that will bind us together."

A long peace pipe that must have been over one hundred years old was lit and passed among us, sitting around the table.

When we got into our LAV, the president shook my hand, "Excellent. I believe we got everything we wanted. We stopped them from leaving the union. Many of their grievances were real. They are ahead in rebuilding. They found a new large field of oil on their territory. They believe they can have the damaged refinery back and running within 60 days. We're going to need all the fuel they can supply. We know the refineries around Houston were all destroyed. All in all, a very productive three days. Based on their agreement to allow us to travel through their land, when can we begin our trip to KC?"

I had to tell the president I knew he wasn't going to like. "Sir, we can leave at any time. However, the mines aren't prepared to accept you. My scouts report there are hundreds of people who took shelter in the mines, there are piles of dead. Many are sick, they drank bad water. We're going to need at least two months to move the people in the mine out, clean the mines, and build rows of simple offices. We also need time to install the secure blast doors. They're actually the leading item. You can't move in without the doors."

"Where did you locate blast doors?"

"Our scout team to Cheyenne Mountain reported while the Russians hit the mountain, they struck the side. The main and internal doors were still intact. The blast pressure vented through the holes in the mountain the Russian's warheads created. Our teams are removing them and making plans for the mines. It's slow work because they have to work in radiation-proof suits that are bulky, heavy, and very hard to work in. We rotate teams around the clock. Their update was they need 45 days to remove the doors, 14 days to carry them to the mines, and 60 days to install them."

"Four months? What happened to change the timeline?"

"Sir, we learned the mines don't have any doors. If they did, they were either blown off or pulled off by people trying to get to any shelter they could."

"General as much as I hate the delay. The good news is that we won't be on the road when we strike the Cartel. How is your little project coming?"

I smiled, knowing the president had a sense of humor and had seen the movie *'Money Pit.'* Sir, two weeks."

He laughed as he punched my arm. "Not funny. But I appreciate the humor. When?"

"Sir. I'll have a better idea when we return, and I can speak to the team in the SCIF."

"I want to see it before you release it."

"Sir, of course."

Chapter 6

Juan Valdez's chief of intelligence told him, "Sir, we have some potentially bad news. The damn Indians have cut a deal with the Yankees."

"Define deal."

"The Indians get to keep New Mexico, and the Yankees agree to leave their hands off the new nation, which they're calling the Native Nation."

Valdez called his council of advisors together to discuss what had happened up north, "My friends, I have just received some wonderful news that I have to share with you. The Yankees have accepted the Indian's demand for their own country. We'll send special teams into the Indian's little nation to cause them so much chaos they'll have to cut a deal with us.

"With the Indians off the board, the Yankees won't have anyone to watch their flank and with their remaining military spread all over what remains of their country we'll be able dictate our terms to the Yankees.

"There's no one the Yankees can call for help, with their traditional allies dead due to the war the Yankees help start. Shortly after Russia invaded Ukraine both sides were willing to sit down and talk. The problem was the Yankees wanted to use this war as a way to destroy the Russian army. Their plan might have worked had they not pushed Putin into a corner leaving him only one way to escape. His only way to win or at least call a cease fire was to first knock NATO back on their heels. He gave them a shock they didn't except and weren't prepared for. Putin had released the nuclear genie from its bottle. This was only the second time the genie had been used in a war.

"The four small tactical nukes would have been enough to get all of the parties to sit at the table because no one wanted the genie to be left out of its bottle. Of course, the crazy Jews had to release their genie on Iran. Don't get me wrong, Iran deserved everything they got but Israel scared the world. NATO and Russia were about to reach a wide-reaching agreement when boom, just like that while the Russian troops were reorganizing and rearming and their troops resting, someone set off a series of nuclear mines. These destroyed most of Russia's army and poisoned the ground. Russian accused NATO who of course accused Russia. This mess got further clouded when the report on where the uranium had been enriched came back, it was from a Russian reactor.

"NATO prepared to strike Russia with all of their nuclear might, that really meant, the Yankees, the Brits and the French. No one knew if the French would really launch their own weapons since they were part-time members of NATO. If NATO adopted a program France didn't approve of then they withdrew from NATO until NATO asked them on bent knees to return. Now mind you, remember in the Second World War, the French had a larger army with more tanks, more guns, more planes, and more of everything than the Germans who conquered France in 7 weeks. The French also lost in Vietnam and in Africa.

"Why am I giving you a little history lesson? Because I want you to understand the loudest dog doesn't always get the bone. Today the Yankees are broken and just beginning to rebuild. I estimate it will take them a full generation for them to where they were, maybe 50 years ago. Their great cities are mass graveyards. Ground Zero under the Russian bombs may be unlivable for more than a generation, and their people will have a deep-seated fear of entering those areas. The Yankees are broken. They are mourning their dead. It may take months or years for them to get out of their period of self-reflection. Many will decide they can't live without their loved ones, and their young have lost their drug of choice, their internet, and that's where we come in.

We will replace their internet with cheap, pure drugs. We don't want our customers to die on us. We want to hook them. Thus, we'll help them by lowering our prices. If their young can't afford our prices, they can always sign up to work for us for a period of five years and receive free drugs. Of course, they'll never go home. Many will die in our fields, the pretty ones will become pleasure girls and then they will OD. If their parents want to talk or see their children who work for us, they'll have to pay us. Those Yankees who think the grass is greener in Mexico can come as long as they can pay our entrance toll. I'm now announcing an increase to fifty thousand for a family of three. If there are more people in the family, then the fee goes up proportionally. If they can't pay the new fees, then they can work the balance off. Soon, one way or another, we'll own the Yankees.

"Some of you believe the Yankees will send their tanks and planes here to crush us. Some of you believe this plan goes far. You're worried our army isn't trained to take on the Yankees during their match-up. I have another surprise for you. In a few weeks, they will have more to fear from us than our drugs. I have made a deal with the North Koreans. They need food and foreign currency. They need fuel, we need weapons. We have the food, fuel, and currency they need. They need a partner for the only things they can export. Military technology and weapons. Just the items we need.

"We know the Yankees will decide we're a direct threat to their rebuilding so they'll come across the border to kill us. They're strike at our fields, at our processing sites, our warehouses, and even our homes. Won't they be surprised when their hundred-million-dollar planes, which can't be reproduced, are shot out of the sky when their tanks are burning from being hit by NK anti-tank missiles that are in reality, Chinese weapons?

"The real surprise I have for the Yankees is I rented 25,000 North Korean troops. An entire division, complete with their weapons, ammo, and their vehicles, including their tanks. Hey Yankee, SURPRISE!

The conference shook from the joy of his advisors, all laughed, some pounded the table, stood and applauded.

"We are going to be in control. We are going to be the world's superpower. Don't like us? We don't care, we get your children hooked on our drugs. Try to attack us, we'll use the missiles and nuclear warheads we purchased from the North Koreans to destroy your country. You can't defeat us. You can't tell what we can and can't do. We hold the rope that's tied around your balls!"

The room was filled with his advisors pounding the table. The servers waiting outside to serve snacks, wine, and beer wondered what was happening in the room. One server who had faithfully served the cartel for five years was in reality, a spy for the CIA. His problem was his handler was dead. He had understood what Valdez had said in the room. It scared him that the heartless cartel was about to be a nuclear-armed state, and that's why they had become an independent state. They controlled Mexico south to South America, and they were making roads to take over SA too. The spy didn't know what to do, no one responded to his emails, and the phone they gave him was dead. He had the largest secret and no one to tell it to.

@@@@@

The President sat in the conference room as the lights dimmed and the wall-sized screen lowered. "General..."

"Mr. President please hold your questions until the program ends."

The program begins with the sight of a row of bulldozers moving piles of debris. The drivers of the bulldozers wore reflective head-to-toe sealed HAZMAT uniforms. The camera zoomed in so the details could be seen. The president said, "That's one of our Minutemen silos, isn't it? Weren't they all destroyed?"

"Sir, please keep watching."

After the debris was cleared the top of the silo open to reveal a torched cylinder where a Minuteman missile had launched. A truck pulled up the silo and a long arm with scrubbing attachments began cleaning the silo. There was a time jump on the show, the camera next showed the clean silo and another truck pull up to the lip of silo. The top of the truck opened and a large white missile was moved into position over the silo. The President watched as the missile was lowered into the silo.

"Sir, this process usually takes hours, we sped it up. To show the Chinese we're really reloading the silos, there's a moving time scale on the bottom of the screen. That will match what they're intelligence will have told them it takes to reload a silo."

"General, are they really reloadable, is this real? I swear it looks like I'm there."

"Sir, I'll address those questions when the program is over."

"Okay, you have my full attention. If this isn't real, it's a hell of a deep fake."

The picture showed two missile control officers in the launch capsule as they checked the recently loaded missile. The president sat up, "I know that's a real launch capsule, I've been in one. How the hell, okay, okay, I'll hold my questions."

The program jumped to a commercial airport and six B-21 Raider stealth bombers. Crewmen were shown loading nuclear bombs into the bomb bay of the bombers.

The program then jumped to another airport where a line of B-1 bombers were being loaded with weapons. This was followed by a sight that made the president stand up and stare at the screen. Two lines of B-52s each was armed with twelve cruise missiles.

The president looked at me and smiled. "Sir, you should enjoy the next clip as well." This time the program the loading of Trident missiles into submarines. It was obvious from the view there were over a hundred-armed Marines protecting the missiles and the loading on the submarine.

The next clip showed a damaged aircraft carrier being repaired by at least four hundred people, men and women installing new deck plates while cranes held new radar antennas being mounted.

"General, are you next going to show me we've brought the battle ships back into service?"

"Only one of them was able to be quickly brought to service, the New Jersey, which gives us two New Jerseys in the fleet."

"General, which parts are real, and which aren't. I couldn't tell."

"Then we might have done a well enough job to convince the Chinese and anyone else we want to warn that we're prepared to respond with hell fire."

"I'd say, your team pulled off an outstanding job. Can you tell me which is real and which is a deep fake?"

"The battleship is real, it will return to the fleet in three months. The BUSH is real, I'm told it can return to the fleet in six months. The B-52s are real. Since most launched stand-off cruise missiles, they were able to return to their backup bases. Of the seventy we sent over, sixty returned, of those ten had battle damage. The trident boats are being reloaded. A hold up is the reserve missiles were located in Virginia in buried weapons bunkers. We had to clear a section of the highway so C-17s could land. Each could only carry two missiles, each boat carried twenty-four missiles and I could only scrape together six C-17s so it's going to take some time to fully reload each of the ten boats that returned from their mission. A little bit of good news is one boat didn't get the EAM to launch. We had to replace her radio and antenna. After we repaired her, she returned to carry out a war patrol.

"Sir, our silos weren't meant to be reused. In the 1960s when they were first designed, the theory was if they ever had to be used, the world would be destroyed. There were wouldn't be a need to reload. The Russians used a cold launch system so their silos could be reloaded. They believed a nuclear war was winnable and it might mean multiple waves of missiles. We used the same process for the Peacekeeper missile, but the missiles were all removed from service. There is a little good news, the Air Force practiced launching Minutemen missiles from C-17s and C-130s. I have a crew working on prepping our existing missiles for plane launch.

"I'm hoping this video which I plan to have shown on the few remaining local stations that are still operating, will convince China we're serious and ready about having to fight them on a nuclear battlefield. I'm editing into the video images of the old civil defense shelter signs here. My team updated them and made them look new. Beijing will believe we quickly made shelters for our survivors, and we're ready to take them on."

The President looked at the images on the screen, and then he looked into my eyes. "Do you think they'll buy it?"

"This combined with flights of B-52s flying to their Failsafe locations just outside of Chinese airspace should convince them we're serious. I'm sending some F-22s with the BUFFs in case some Chinese fighters come up to play. Their orders are to knock down anyone interfering with the bombers."

"Okay, I'll take your word. In the meantime, you need to speed up the transfer of power to KC. Time might be running out."

"Sir, now that we have reached an agreement with the Indians, I've ordered Captain Rand to continue to KC with all due haste. Once he meets up with our advance scouts, then I'll have a better handle on when we can get you moved to the mines. We're working a plan to mount other doors to seal the mines so you can move in earlier than we had discussed."

"General, please hurry. I have a real bad feeling about the future."

"Yes, sir."

End of Book 1

The story will continue in Book 2

Additional books by the author are available on Amazon:

NATO's Article 5 Gambit Book 1
NATO's Article 5 Gambit Book 2 (Coming fall 2023)

Buddy can you spare a few Trillion? (Coming Spring 2023)

Behind Every Blade of Grass book 1
Behind Every Blade of Grass book 2,
Behind Every Blade of Grass book 3
Behind Every Blade of Grass book 4
Behind Every Blade of Grass book 5
Behind Every Blade of Grass book 6
Behind Every Blade of Grass book 7
Behind Every Blade of Grass book 8
Behind Every Blade of Grass book 9
Behind Every Blade of Grass book 10

The Smoky Mountain Militia (A story set in the Behind Every Blade of Grass universe.)
Fighting Behind Enemy Lines. (Coming summer 2023.) (A story set in the Behind Every Blade of Grass universe.)

The Wrath of God, Book 1
The Wrath of God, Book 2

Red Sunset.
Earthquake
Pestilence
Pax Romana

It's Good to be the King. Book 1
It's Good to be the King, Book 2

The Changelings Book 1
Justin's Journal
Project Xiangqi
Korean Crises

CALEXIT, Book 1, Secession
CALEXIT, Book 2, Politics as Normal.
CALEXIT, book 3, If at First, You Don't Secede

America on Fire

37 Miles (Revised Edition)
37 Miles, Book 2, Patty's Journey

My Story
A History Lesson (Short story)

2015 Second American Civil War, Book 1
2015 Second American Civil War, Book 2
2015 Second American Civil War, Book 3
2015 Second American Civil War, Book 4
2015 Second American Civil War, Book 5

By the Light of the Moon, Book 1
By the Light of the Moon, Book 2
By the Light of the Moon, Book 3
By the Light of the Moon, Book 4

Christmas Eve

The Shelter, Book 1, The Beginning
The Shelter, Book 2, A Long Day's Night
The Shelter, Book 3, The Aftermath
The Shelter, Book 4, The New World.
The Shelter, Book 5, War
The Shelter, Book 6, Revenge
The Shelter, Book 7, Genesis
The Shelter, Chapter 2, a new beginning.

In the Year 2050, America's Religious Civil War
In the Year 2050, Book 2

The Impeachment of President Obama
Silent Death
The Third World War

We Knew They Were Coming, Book 1
We Knew They Were Coming, Book 2
We Knew They Were Coming, Book 3
We Knew They Were Coming, Book 4
We Knew They Were Coming, Book 5
We Knew They Were Coming, Book 6
We Knew They Were Coming, Book 7
We Knew They Were Coming, Book 8
We Knew They Were Coming, Book 9
We Knew They Were Coming, Book 10

Feel free to contact me at itabankin@aol.com with any questions or comments.

Printed in Great Britain
by Amazon